FIC   Kondoleon, Harry.
           Diary of a lost boy.

$19.50

DATE			

JUL   1994

BAKER & TAYLOR BOOKS

DIARY OF A LOST BOY

DIARY OF
A LOST BOY

—

a novel by

Harry Kondoleon

Alfred A. Knopf *New York*

19 🐆 94

THIS IS A BORZOI BOOK
PUBLISHED BY ALFRED A. KNOPF

Copyright © 1993 by Harry Kondoleon
All rights reserved under International and Pan-American
Copyright Conventions. Published in the United States
by Alfred A. Knopf, Inc., New York, and simultaneously in
Canada by Random House of Canada Limited, Toronto.
Distributed by Random House, Inc., New York.

Library of Congress Cataloging-in-Publication Data
Kondoleon, Harry.
Diary of a lost boy : a novel / by Harry Kondoleon.
p.   cm.
ISBN 0–679–43067–9
1. Marriage—New York—Fiction.   2. AIDS (Disease)—
Fiction.   3. New York (N.Y.)—Fiction.
I. Title.
PS3561.0456d5   1994
813'.54—dc20   93–24257
                                   CIP

Manufactured in the United States of America
First Edition

to my friends

ACKNOWLEDGMENTS

*The author gratefully acknowledges
the contributions of M. Elizabeth Osborn
and Stephen Soba.*

DIARY OF A LOST BOY

For the soul has strange guests with whom it is conversing.

MEISTER ECKHART

——

On Detachment

I don't know how much to include and how much to leave out.

If I'd truly attained detachment, I would see no difference in the fact my doctor on Tuesday said I had two years to live (at most) and the fact my best friend Susan Ded's marriage is falling apart. What's more important?

The other problem in beginning is to begin; in beginning, all endings begin. So, in effect, the end is nearest at the beginning. I mean, when I finish I'll be kaput. There'll be no more me at the end;

I'll be so . . . gone. And perhaps Susan will be re-married—rematched, anyway.

My failure at detachment reaches me tonight in my tub water. A strangulation. It isn't the intensity of my new bath product that chokes me, or even the high heat of the water. It is the Despair Factor, oh so delicately squeezing the neck. Friend, if you have never woken up and not known what your purpose in life might be, read no further. To care so much about the Deds' marriage is weird in the extreme; after all, they didn't marry me. And Bill Ded isn't even a very interesting man. Still, I suppose, he isn't as pathetic as I've become, and I do hate to see marriages fall apart.

There's nothing more revolting than a not-too-well-groomed man over thirty-five.

KARL LAGERFELD

———

On Death and Detachment

Forgive me if you've heard this story before; I've been telling it all over town. The doctor who first diagnosed me (not the one I have now) was very grim on the subject of recovery. A downhill slide at varying speeds for varying individuals was his most optimistic offering. Soon after, he fell over dead, and was discovered by his wife, who was left widowed with a group of fatherless children. The doctor's death created a stir in the weight-maintenance community, because his shape would change radically via diet pills. His wife hates when I tell this story because, at the expense of the doctor, it teaches his life-threatened patients the nature of irony.

For example, Susan. Susan was dating a lot of not very nice men, and I felt finally I had to intercede. I introduced her to Bill, they married, and before long suspicious details concerning Bill's fidelity emerged and the marriage suffered serious decay. The end is yet in sight. On the other hand, look at me. Even though I'm considered half-dead, I sit in my living doctor's waiting room making goo-goo eyes at the attractive, but probably also half-dead, men.

I'm adjusting my amusing new hat, drawing attention to my interesting shoes. Then I catch sight of myself in my little mind's eye and I have to laugh.

This is something you will have to adjust to, the laugh of my mind's eye. It is a sour detail in an otherwise pleasant personality. "Don't be a fool" is the gist of its campaign. It won't be satisfied until every coffin lid is snapped shut. I have gone to countless crackpot psychiatrists to quiet this indignant voice. What can I do?

The new doctor has what he advertises as more bad news.

"Your blood's worse—much worse. Everything's down," he says, his glee partially hidden behind substantiating lab reports.

Liar, I think.

"You look bad. Are you walking? Getting any sunlight? Food?"

"Oh yes, definitely."

The "You look bad" is a low blow. I pull some

various hairs in different directions across my head. How bad could I look? It isn't even twelve-thirty yet.

Another asshole is the Deds' doorman. Whenever I enter the building I get his "you again" expression. He says "They're out" exactly the way my doctor's receptionist says "Your bill." Someone should do a documentary film on his rudeness.

The Ded apartment is surprisingly plain. Corridors that burst onto large rooms. White. Unphenomenal marquetry. Some art from the larger Ded collection, Bill's parents'. I don't mind sitting there waiting for Susan or Bill to appear. As I've already established, my ego is a diminished entity. So I'm not so fascinating; so what. At least I feel responsible for my actions. I got Bill and Susan together, and since the results have been less than felicitous, I do feel I have some responsibility to set it right one way or another before I die.

Susan and I went to the same college, a beautiful complexity among giant maple trees. I loved what I considered her urban flamboyance. I'd gone to a high school where there was a stampede of athletic activities, and I longed for poetry and art. Susan could write and draw a little, and she had strong opinions. Strong opinions, I feel, are a kind of creativity. Later, after Susan took some hard knocks from love's fuck-you agenda, her opinions became less vivid.

"Darling, I don't believe you're taking any of this seriously enough! Think of what your doctor has told you! Can't you see this turn of events demands you take some action? And you want to sit there and chat about my stupid marriage as if it mattered a bug in the scheme of things? You're my dear friend and I want to be there for you. And even though we both know Bill's a bastard, he's there for you too. Oh, darling!"

"Don't scold me, Susan."

I was not yet prepared to tell her about my budding commitment to detachment. I wasn't ready to say yes, death is large and its cheerless theater dark, but I am determined now to enlarge upon the attendant despair and make a home of detachment. Death, inevitably, our second residence.

All creatures are pure nothingness. I do not say they are small or petty: they are pure nothingness.

——

The Let's-Do-Nothing Club

Once Bill found out about my predicament he decided to be of help.

He took me to his Philandering Husbands Support Group. The support group baffled me. Was it a group to help curtail sexually compulsive behavior, or was it more of what it said it was, a club for husbands who wanted to be supported in their philandering?

Many of the men in the club were in the process of divorce but, oddly, were adamant about not ever using the word. They would insist they were merely "separated." "It's a separation," a philanderer shouted to the other fellows.

It was a not particularly attractive group of men. But I have to admit the majority of their stories about sneaking around for sex were very sexy. I couldn't help admiring the ingenuity and the downright Jacobean backdrop of guilt and self-loathing. Clearly, Bill had informed the crowd of my own situation. I was afforded a wide berth in every way. There were no other homosexuals in the crowd; that was clarified by the zealous description of their expeditions. They loved Secret Vagina and would find no way to halt their enthusiasm. I won't be unfair and say they looked at me with pity. I was an Other, and they would tolerate, even welcome, a visitor from a foreign planet, providing I did not squirt alien fluid in their direction.

The support group reminded me of an unfortunate club I joined in the fourth grade. Sex United. A silly, small organization of fourth-grade boys who, to maintain membership status, were required to bring in any sex-related nonsense culled from magazines and newspapers. It was a pansexual organization without knowing it. Photos of male movie stars standing outside their hotel rooms with slight erections beneath their bath towels, as well as female movie stars brazenly dropping their towels on the boardwalks of Cannes, were admissible. The club inevitably disintegrated (evolved?) into a kind of wrestling club, and membership fell off when older siblings labeled its chatter perversion.

Frankly, I could not fully grasp the name Sex

United. Then it was explained to me that it simply referred to a penis being *in* a vagina so they were *united*. Well, it seems so obvious now, but at the time I was confused.

Although I know Bill had spoken previously of my poor health, he leapt up to give me an embarrassing introduction. "We'll help any way we can!" rallied Bill. You can well imagine the bewildered expressions of the philanderers. What could they do? As nonhomosexuals, they could not at this late date reinterpret how sex should be united. One intelligent member set forth the forthright notion that a lot of their promiscuity was probably based on an avoidance of death, so it would be difficult for them to honestly embrace one so clearly earmarked for doom. I respected him and admired the way his suit clung to his chest and thighs.

I'd started to dress like a pregnant woman in her third trimester: very large things with balls of Kleenex in all the pockets. I don't believe any of my eccentricities were judged harshly. Because the philanderers came together in a confederacy of shame and chauvinism, they couldn't very well care what I was wearing. Anyway, I probably very much fit their idea of what a modern homosexual was about.

"I'm a shit, I'm a shit, I'm a shit," a husband proclaimed.

"You mustn't say that," I said, trying to be encouraging. But, in fact, after he listed all the twisted assignations that had tortured and embarrassed his family, I could agree there was something feceslike about his character.

I'm certain that when I was entreated to speak of my sex life, I disappointed the majority who had far fiercer footnotes to their phallic histories. I won't lie and say I was condescended to; no, the philanderers were not hypocrites. They did ask my permission to bring a prostitute in for one session, and I properly volunteered to stay home.

Later, deeper into my disintegration, I joined another group. It was in no way based on the naughty husbands club and lacked totally its joy in self-flagellation.

In my mind, for I dared not identify it as such out loud, I called this group the Let's-Do-Nothing Club. It was originally organized as an opportunity for fellow sufferers to run over the miserable mistakes of their doctors and the perils of the disease. But that ran thin, and soon a capacious silence sat on the room.

Let me tell you, because it's no joke: this was a mysterious club with a vanishing membership; members would die and they wouldn't come back. Yes, many of us were visiting hospitals for spalike spans of time, but that was to be expected. It was the Xeroxes that created violent quiet. Suddenly someone would not be at a meeting. Suddenly you would look over your shoulder and there, on the wall, would be a Xerox of a photo of a recently deceased group member.

"Patrick died," someone might say to accompany the blatancy of the Xerox.

Before Patrick disappeared he was, for me, a source both of ego fulfillment and its grim cousin futility. I don't know why, but whenever I chose to speak, my simple words were greeted with great enthusiasm. It was a little embarrassing, effortlessly reaching guru status.

"Hector's right. I agree with Hector. Hector's right." What did I say?

Eventually, I had to admit to myself there was some pleasure in having my small thoughts and admonishments to stay brave held up for praise.

Patrick said, "When I go home I think all week of what Hector said."

All week.

So when they brought the Xerox of Patrick to pin upon the wall, with baseball hat and simple grin . . . you understand?

Susan only half understood the silence of the Let's-Do-Nothing Club.

She had been part of her own noisy club when she discovered Bill was a philanderer. She screamed out, "I'm destroyed! Destroyed!" Then she proceeded to call her closest girlfriends and demand they come over, even leave work—and why? "Because I'm destroyed!" Those who were curious enough about this state of being—and more than you'd estimate were—came over.

Susan, crying, explained how discovering Bill's infidelities all at once made her lose confidence in reality. After all, if she could be so wrong about her marriage, what else was she off on? Slowly everyone was confessing her own bitter disappointments and humiliating concessions.

She would paste herself back together, she'd see.

Let's hear no more of this "destroyed" word. Since nature was quick to destroy everything anyway it was silly to assist that process in any way.

The fact that I was sitting there didn't seem to affect anyone, even though I had no husband who telephoned whores or who had a student girlfriend (seventeen!) or fellow office workers who in lieu of the gym exercised a rough leisure after work.

The women calmed down after a while—except one woman, who threw herself on the floor but then said, "I forgot what I was going to say." A discussion on changing the carpet took over, and the woman on the floor had the best vantage point.

I didn't want everything to get so parodistic. I didn't want to be such an isolated character. Even if I was going to drop dead quickly, I wanted some feelings of being integrated among my fellow beings. Even a romance: someone to kiss tenderly and expressively. Modern, I took these feelings of vague hurt to a therapist. Bold of me too, since I'd had a history of nut therapists. I didn't know until I was told that nuttiness went with the territory, that people already having brain problems felt their own agonies would offer them insight into other sufferers.

"I'm an HIV expert!" said the therapist. Here we go again, I said to myself.

At a first session I always like to come up with something good. Something that sums up all my despair and malformed affections. Something *shrinkable*.

Avoiding parent-related grievances, I went for a

rather curt tale of how in the fifth grade I was asked to deliver a note from one teacher to another and upon entering the foreign classroom was greeted with the warlike cry of a student extrapolating, "He's a girl!"

I'm lying. This never happened to me (although God knows it could have!) but to a friend, a friend now gone who perhaps in shady eternity must endure the derisive laughter of nasty children, apprentice devils. I return often to this scene and, in honor of my friend, I interject my present-day persona and scold the laughing class:

"Reverse your treacherous hearts! Renounce the antilove movement! Villainous children of the damned, future ghosts, baboons, apologize!" And so forth.

The therapist says, "Leave your bitterness behind," but it sounds like she's asking who has the bitterest behind.

I already know what God will say when I confront him about what an unjust and monster-filled world he oversees: "It's *supposed* to be that way," in a schoolyard baby voice. Oh, God, why could you not have had a more sophisticated sense of humor and made everything happy? Who could ever forgive you now?

—

Weather

Feeling of time closing in. Not very nice. The weather. February. Mean and white. But a birthday month—talisman against death. Health much worse. Doctor confirms. Waiting room filled with old women; where are all the gay men?

Whistle while you wait.

Death arrives like a pig in a blanket, like a carrot in a pot, salted, salted. A nobody at a party. A big nobody, death. Emily of Emily Dickinson fame rolls on the carpet. She's been jilted from an intense affair, imagination on fire, big secret. I'm nobody now, nobody nobody nobody.

Oh, dear Emily, please don't take it seriously. I will distract you by describing the weather. My taxi rides up the road that goes along the river—we still have rivers—and the surface moves like a teenager at a first rock-'n'-roll party. Cold crests, smoke, Clorox sky, angel surveillance. Look at me: I'm a cloudy day when you've misplaced all your valuables. Hotel with no one at the desk. The doctor wants me to try another drug. "Sound more confident," I want to say. Tell him, he says, if it makes me dizzy and sick. Okay. Tell him if it makes the bottoms of my feet numb. Okay. Tell him if insomnia comes.

Oh, it comes.

Middle of the night, decorative snowflakes tonight, rose clouds under black veils, gas of cold weather, argument in the street, she's through with him treating her like shit—"It's over, over, over!" she says.

Morning is worse. Snow says "I am a hallucination" and disappears.

Too cold to go out. Pharmacy won't deliver. Wander from room to room. No faith. Air conditioner implies with benign quiet we will be friends again this August (at the latest). I turn it on now to spite the weather. Radiator such an overachiever the room never gets cold. I turn off the air conditioner. I'm mean and white like the weather. Vladimir Nabokov criticizes Fyodor Dostoevsky for his lack of description of weather. I'm careful not to fall into that trap.

The sin against hope—the deadliest sin and perhaps also the most cherished, the most indulged. It takes a long time to become aware of it, and the sadness which precedes and heralds its advent is so delicious! The richest of all the devil's elixirs, his ambrosia.

GEORGES BERNANOS

——

This Corpse for Hire

Why do I go on about the Deds? I hope it is not the syndrome of the single gay man projecting himself into the straight couple or straight man or straight woman. I was friends with them before I was diagnosed. I helped find them their apartment. They love me. They see after me.

When Susan is trying on something new or seeing if something old still fits, she will take everything off, underwear and all, and stand naked in front of me. I don't comment on this habit. Her body is female perfection. She gazes in the mirror, the immodesty of a new goddess. I don't feel like the invisible man. Bill has often invited me to his health club. In the steam room he seems eager to display himself, slapping various muscle groups to check their progress. I hesitate to add this because, again, I don't want to fall into any gay stereotype, but the detail is too interesting to delete: he has a gorilla penis. He lets it swing in the steam room and, although it is a largely straight health club, there are a fair number of bug-eyed creatures who seem quite prepared to lunge.

I have never watched them make love, but somehow I believe they might like that.

Oh, what's all this Adam and Eve bullshit! I'm involved with the Deds because I feel there's no more me, or just a me disappearing.

"But we're all disappearing."

"Yes, but not on such a tight schedule."

"I'm not going to listen anymore when you say blatantly negative things. I don't mind being there for you when you're down, but I won't sponge up a lot of negativity."

"The red one."

"It's almost burgundy. Not too tight across the bust?"

"In a good way."

"And you know what I could wear with it? Those old, weird-heeled suede shoes that never really went in or out of style."

"Frizon, Maud."

And so it goes: death is kicked by overpriced shoes—in this case, shoes that have waited patiently in the closet for their day. And now, with the purchase of the tight red (not quite burgundy, a dark magenta . . . the blood of a recent transfusion . . . *oui!*) dress, the shoes will emerge like an underrated artist.

"Oh, Susan, clothes look so good on you!"

"Don't talk phony to me. I can tell. You're at your blackest when you take that tone. Not with me!"

I admire that, I guess. It's why I keep coming back and sitting in the lobby, waiting because the Doorman (dog trainer to Cerberus) says he can't find the spare key.

"Don't pity me," I whisper, but the Doorman doesn't hear me, he's busy insulting people on the intercom. ("Oh, Mrs. *Gross,* it's the Doorman, those flowers you said would be delivered today never came! I thought you'd like to know.")

Yes, I'm quiet today, waiting in the lobby of the catacombs. I've chosen a chilly, anti-Castaneda spot, comfortless physically and spiritually. It is on this cushion I can chart the death of Hope. It is the death of Hope that makes me come here. Rather than even attempt the funeral or memorial service, I will help set the table for a little dinner party I refuse to attend. Yes, the Deds are still entertaining, even though, for now, Bill sleeps in the living room on the couch (one of several couches).

"When did your sense of a future abandon you?" asks the therapist. This one is free and comes right to your apartment. She is one of the gingerbread mamas who look at you gooey with raisin eyes.

I don't know when Hope died, because I guess

I didn't want to look. I don't suspect it was a grisly death: skin removed in gradations, guts strewn, bones flung, blood gone. It must have been more sudden: slipping out a window, a dunking from a pier. So many poets have celebrated the death of Hope. I can't do that. It was a little but loyal friend. I didn't know when it died there would be just this shell of me left. I didn't know I would be the corpse so soon and prematurely.

"You must not have a job," says the Doorman. "I wish I had your free time. You're not one of those AIDS persons, are you?"

It's my turn now to play deaf.

"I ask because you have that little spot on your face."

I thought I'd applied a sufficient amount of the cover-up Susan had run out and bought for me the second we spotted the purple spot.

"You should see Mr. Andrews in 11-C. I call him Spotty! He has the courage to go out."

An attractive woman enters the building with a slightly younger man. They are laughing uproariously. I know they are going up to have sex. The elevator door shuts. "What's so funny to them?" says the Doorman, put out by their sex appeal. In the house of the Deds everyone is certainly not dead.

Susan rushes in with a cartoon quantity of shopping bags, all from stores you don't imagine anyone shopping in.

"Darling, forgive me, I had all kinds of credit-card and cab problems—I'm late."

"He was early," assists the Doorman.

We take the elevator. Still perfumed, funky.

"Do you smell the elevator?" I ask Susan.

"The whole building smells as far as I'm concerned. Before I unofficially placed Mr. Bill in the world of the unliving we were discussing a country house. I figured I'd spend all my time there. Ha. But I wish I had it now. I could take care of you there. Your bedroom could be on the first floor so you wouldn't have to deal with stairs."

We go through the shopping bags, more bags than shopping. Bill enters suddenly. No agreement has been reached about who will move out, who will vaporize, who will forgive, who will talk.

"Hector, tell Susan I'll be away all weekend with Bob. We're going to see a house he's representing— lake, pool with little waterfall, three guest rooms, one on the main floor, Hector."

"Hector, please tell the as-far-as-I'm-concerned-dead Mr. Ded that he must be out of his fucking mind to think I give a flying fuck where he spends this weekend or any fucking weekend forthcoming."

"Hector, do me a favor and inform my frigid wife that if she should decide to have another angry women's meeting here she might consider having someone in to help clear the empty liquor bottles and smoky air."

"Fuck yourself!"

That message was given directly, and I see Bill to the door with his weekend bag. We kiss on the cheek. I know Susan is facedown, crying. She loves

Bill so much. I must sign them up for a seminar on how men and women love differently. I saw the flyer at the Open Center.

When I get back to my own apartment and happen to pass a mirror, it's a bit shocking, because I see the corpse. But of course, this is where the corpse lives! A recent graduate, it doesn't stink yet. It actually takes some years before complete putrefaction. I think I see it twitch! No, a truck passed and the mirror shook. Shifty cadaver. I drag it into another room. Heavier than unhappiness, dead Hope. No, I cannot spend the night here. My false smile engenders worms. My beauty went to the circus to apply for a job.

I take a cab back to Susan.

"Out cruising?" says the cab driver as if testing his ESP.

At the building the Doorman is still there, sleeping standing up, and just as I pass him noiselessly his eyes flash open and he laughs and laughs and laughs.

Susan meets me at the door as if she'd summoned me.

"Sleep with me tonight, baby," she says without looking me in the eye. There's no ambivalence about what she means. I'm the lost brother to cuddle with in the shelter from the storm. In bed, she cries and cries. I cry too, just as much.

"What happened to the dinner party?" I remember suddenly.

"Cancelled, cancelled, cancelled, cancelled . . ."

> No fact in human nature is more characteristic
> than its willingness to live on a chance.
>
> WILLIAM JAMES

——

Monster Dinner Party,

Zombie Weekend

A week later, a turn in the plot. Another dinner party. Whereas my attendance was previously optional, I am being told I must attend this one and look my best. If I didn't know better I would believe some matchmaking effort was in effect. I don't know better; it is.

Bill and Susan have even called some temporary truce to make this happen. I'm enlisted to select the menu and vote for which mutually hating people can be placed at the same table. I choose their other best friends, also estranged and fed-up, although less volatile than the hosts. Shrimp cocktail, crab claws, lobster. I decide on a shellfish medley only because the Chinese herbalist (who prescribed a tea that blackened my teeth) prohibited their consumption, saying, "Poison, dirty, no!" For dessert, ice cream sundaes, because everyone likes them. For flowers, alarmist red tulips with intense inner mouths of black and yellow. Antique tablecloth embroidered with bluets. James Robinson silver. Better-quality white embossed plates from Pottery Barn. Candles that twist on their way up, amazing little wheelchair ramps to the place of the flame.

We discuss salad.

Perversely, we decide on chopped-up little fruits with red cabbage and nuts and tart vinegar.

She will have this homely teenaged girl in to help. She's reliable, so Susan won't have to worry about scarring her new red dress. All shellfish will be shell-free, although intuition doesn't tell her she may be needing the claws.

Who's coming? Bill's best friend and fellow philanderer and charter club member, Bob. His wife, Aileen, who, prone, criticized the carpet, a semi-friend of Susan's. And Susan's dear friend and magazine bigwig, Mag, and her mysterious (in a creepy way) husband, Kent. Besides the warring hosts, there's me and the set-up-but-casually friend of Someone or Other.

Someone or Other's friend has been loosely described as a specimen of divine beauty, a regular Greek, Olympian variety. I'm to be awed by his multiple attributes and maybe even, as a result, delete my name from the misery index.

Here's where the comedy grows as rich as French pastry, as deep as the aroma from a pot-au-feu—anyway, anything French and superior.

The pot-au-feu enters, whom we will call Max Drake, because that in fact is his real name. It would be too sticky to sit here and describe the Drake's beauty; it is complete in every visible detail. He even speaks eloquently, yet with no pretensions. He's refined, well mannered, a full, rich laugh informed by intelligence and human kindness. Just the kind of person I ordinarily would like to set fire to.

But here's the twist. Instead of clamming up, I'm charming and witty and surprisingly alive! We seem to be having a real rapport. His good looks swell during the main course. His appeal does not shrivel in the way of so many who have stayed for dessert.

I think I know what this is about. It is too perfect otherwise, too evil: the shot ghosts from roulette toying with my sense of Chance. (A relative of Hope, Chance is less feminine, more ballsy, but less likely to win.) My heart is intended to roll away the stone and I'm to emerge from the dank crypt into the bright new Easter of love.

Only it's not to be that kind of dinner party. While I'm busy being so scintillating, the other side of the table is bickering.

"Must you push your food with your fingers, Bob? When I'm out with you I feel like I'm with my son instead of a husband."

Bob responds, "Well, Aileen, that's very revealing, how your mothering impulses have smothered this marriage and erased any erotic potential it may have ever had."

"And Susan, what's with all the shellfish? You know I can't eat shellfish. I'm allergic. And I would think certain medically compromised guests might have been considered."

"Oh, shut up, Aileen, with your stupid superiority!"

"Don't talk to her that way!"

"I'm used to it."

"You can serve all the shellfish in the world and still be serving pig at the table so long as there's a man present," says Magazine Mag, appetite intact.

"Sexist bullshit."

"All of them man haters," Kent says.

"Kent the zombie speaks."

"That's cruel!"

"I don't care."

"No, he doesn't care about much of anything. Do you, Kent? Maybe that's the secret of our marriage; not giving a damn becomes a kind of loyalty."

"By the way, Bill, I met one of your tarts in the street yesterday. Quite a mess I found her. Has she gone professional?"

"Not half as messy as the fruit tart we're supposed to consume for dessert. Peeked at it in the kitchen—looks like scrambled brains."

"It was twenty-five dollars."

"Which tart are you referring to?"

"Desserts are a little redundant after you've served candied carrot buttons! For a minute I thought it was Christmas in Alabama."

"Susan, what's the point of this dinner party? You and Bill aren't talking. We all hate each other in our own ways, that's obvious, and I have this weird feeling Bill's trying some matchmaking maneuver with Hector but in typical male dodo style he has failed to mention Max here is engaged to be married *to a woman*. Yes, his decade-long bisexuality may have thrown you, but, my man, catch up with the news!"

Instead of this outburst embarrassing Maxwell, he just looks sheepishly around the room, as if his powers of attraction were not something he could ever be held accountable for.

Rather than change my personality to accommodate this new information, I merely bump up the works a little higher, as if this were the best news anyone could have hoped for: "Congratulations!" I keep saying. A spring wedding! A spring wedding!

It's interesting how easily the nightmare version of yourself can emerge after a slight electrical alteration in the reality.

"I have exciting news too!" I say, loud. "I got my latest T-cell count. You all know by this point what that is—a kind of sports record of how your immune system is doing during your last inning. I'm zero! A whole zero. Everyone else at the table probably has something as high as a thousand. Oh, Max, I'm so sorry—I don't know you as well as everyone else at the table and I may have shocked you. We didn't share any needles, but then we did dip our shrimp in the same cocktail sauce—perfectly safe, we're assured."

"Please be quiet, Hector."

"Ooh, I guess that last transfusion gave me just a tad too much energy. It's true I was more manageable as Grandpa, and now I've become a Day-Glo Gidget—keep me away from the candles, I'll go up in flames!"

"The evening is finished—goodnight, everyone. I'll call you on the telephone," Susan says.

I say, "Reminds me of *The Glass Menagerie* when Amanda says, 'Things have a way of working out so badly. . . .'" Everyone is up and out when I get to Amanda Wingfield's outcry "We've been entertaining someone else's fiancé!"

I'm terribly afraid I'm borderline-shrieking now, so I cover my face. I haven't been very *cool*. I turned so quickly from charm-school Dracula to crucifixion screamer.

I don't remember leaving the table. I go into the guest room, strip, and crawl into the bed. I haven't brushed or flossed my teeth . . . oh well, I guess I just won't have my own teeth in old age!

I hear Susan and Bill fiddling away in the next room.

They are making love. No talking. I guess by not saying anything to each other they can continue to be angry. When they're through, Bill regains his couch bed. I'm in no position to judge heterosexual affinities or their accompanying discord. Overheard (from the din of my charms) dinner conversation, banal-hostile variety, contempt in eleven shades of grayness. But then, I feel I've flambéed it royally with my queen routine. The only person who comes off admirable is Mr. Perfect, who excused himself so gracefully it is impossible to take offense.

I feel like I've been licking the bottom of a fish tank. I can't remember what was dessert. Embarrassment *aux noisettes*.

The day after the no-one-will-clean-the-table dinner party is a Saturday, and then there's a Sunday too. It's a zombie weekend. Almost silent.

I take out my injection materials because it's time to give myself my daily shot but more so to inspire inquiry or conversation from Bill or Susan.

It doesn't work. Neither the ploy nor perhaps the injections. Supposed to increase my red or white blood cells, I forget which. Hold the refrigerated vial of clear solution; rub little vial to get it to body temperature; flip top off; rub top with alcohol to sterilize; unwrap injection needle; remove protective needle encasement; turn vial upside down; stick needle into rubber top of vial; withdraw needle's pump, being mindful not to get any air from the vial into the needle's solution. Rub designated skin area with alcohol prep pad; stick in needle; pump solution into flesh; remove and dispose of needle; rub area again with alcohol to prevent swelling and blot any blood that may have beaded at the skin surface.

This procedure having earned no inquiries, I resort to reviewing (again) the ghastly dinner party. The magazine editor had the brass balls to ask if she might arrange a piece on me, "struggling with a terminal disease but with humor." Bob, although I know him quite well from the straight support group, stared at me as if fascinated to see a real homo in action. True, I was practically entwined (emotionally) around the Gentleman Caller; still, it needn't be observed with the wonder of Planet of the Apes. And although Susan is my best friend, she does this weird thing where she sort of pretends she doesn't know me. Bill was semisolicitous. Showing remarkable tact, he skips asking me his usual "Have you remembered to take your pills?"

Whom have I left out? I suppose I can't adequately describe the guests because they are not entirely real to me. When I cease to be entirely real to myself, some kind of liberation will have taken place.

Papers arrive. *Fashions of the Times.* Exposed midriffs. Tulle cover-ups. Lazy mules. Other sections barely touched. A terror of knowing any more than will get us through the weekend. Terrible wind outside. A tortured pet. We walk from room to room as if we cannot see each other. We have tacitly agreed not to acknowledge the absurdity of *trying*. The Deds making love angry is a kind of trying, but a little bit ugly. My trying to forget that I'm out of the game and a bit absurd as a result is ugly too in its manifestation, no matter how gently ugly, and worthy of sympathy. The withered (so soon!) tulips are ugly too, folding into themselves, crinkled lips, limp stamens, murky water. Smelly lobster remains.

Monday blood tests await me. Blood, blood, and more blood. The industry of blood. The world of blood. Commodities. Liabilities. Zest.

Is zest the grated skin of a citrus fruit? I think so. Has made itself present of late, this zest.

"I keep it to a minimum," reports Bianca Jagger, "whether I'm going on a fact-finding mission in Nicaragua or away on holiday. I use skin-care products by Janet Sartin."

MAGAZINE

——

AZT, CMV, DDI, KS,
MAI, PCP, XYZ

I use some scrap paper I find in the doctor's waiting room to compose some thank-you notes.

Dear Mr. Drake:
    What a treat it was to meet someone so
bright and winning. A real thrill! Your necktie
was stunning. All I can say is your fiancée is
a very lucky girl! Hey, go fuck yourself!

I throw that away.

Dear Max:
    Darling, can't you see we are made for each
other? I fear the chaos of the party last night

might have obscured the vision of what I see as
our blissful life together. Don't bother sending
me red roses, just jot down BE MINE and
messenger it over. We will always be true to
each other. What could ever separate two so
devoted?

Your Own Little Hector

I throw that away too and work on a general one
for the other guests.

Dear Other People at the Dinner Party the
Other Night:
    Do you even exist? How dare you look at me
while I breathe, imagining me an inevitable
imminent hole in the scenery? It was practically
audible, your consensual thinking: We'll be here
next year and he won't. It was all too clear, your
giddy eagerness for my demise. No, I'm not
being paranoid; I know how off-putting it is for
the well to be seated next to the unwell with all
the ramifications of pain and death. And don't
pity me for my pathetic display of desire. I just
sincerely hope Mr. Drake's lovely fiancée (why
didn't he bring her, the ambivalent asshole?)
has attained the appropriate lab reassurances.
I wish you all luck and lots of it because it is
horrendously obvious that is what we all require
in this grisly world. Amen.

I let this other letter drift to the floor. Autumn
leaf on loam. The desk nurse says, "Your turn now,"
with predictable ominousness.
    The doctor is running from office to office as if it

were Christmas Eve at Morgan Guaranty. He finally settles down to review my folder, my alphabet history.

"You were on AZT for how long?"

"Three years."

"But with no anemia, right?"

"Right."

Why must we continually review the same material, month after month?

"But then you got the PCP and detected your first KS lesions."

He's a tutor.

"That's correct."

"And the MAI."

"And the CMV."

"So I have you on the DDI. What are we doing for the CMV? DHPG?"

"Right."

And so on. I guess it would be okay if the doctor spoke with some degree of authority. You know, something like "This is *really* going to work!" The way they do at ritzy pharmacies while pushing their overpriced moisturizer. But it's too much, the epidemic; they *don't know*. Difficult to be sympathetic.

And then I have this new therapist who I think is just a social worker; anyway. She seems adamant that I understand this is a *terminal* illness. As if I didn't know.

"There's so much *denial* in the AIDS community." This is her big thing. Perhaps nonstop screaming would adequately demonstrate a lack of denial and—

Anyway, I'm supposed to be concentrating on detachment.

Mercedes vs. jalopy. Bel Air vs. Red Hook. Where is it easier to be detached? Lutèce or Burger King? Majorca or in an empty garage?

Disinterestedness.

New prescriptions to fill. Insurance company calls to say I've used up more than three-quarters of my lifetime allotment of insurance and do I want to switch to pay out-of-pocket?

"No," I say.

I go to the Deds. They aren't home and I go through their two closets. No reason; just to touch and feel, pinch the fabrics, make judgments, time passing.

The refrigerator has spoiling leftovers. I eat a Freezer Pop and watch television. A commercial for a film generally intended for children but not exclusively says, "Be afraid. Be very afraid."

I am afraid. I'm afraid you're thinking, Well, what went wrong with this character? To get to this dark depot? He's being awfully mum about past relationships, romantic or otherwise. What kind of bad career choices did he make? Are his parents still alive? Was the childhood very arduous?

I am afraid these scrappy bits are going by in the wind very fast. If I stay at the Deds' apartment I won't have to think. In my own apartment the unraveling would be very speedy. But without witness. If I concentrate on helping them through their marriage difficulties, I can kid death out of looking me directly in the eyes; you know what he's like. My little muffin, he says, my little friend from life, come now, pet, we will walk my black beach together, and when the inky water closes over your head, I'll be there, yes, all the laughing will be over but we'll be together for a very long time.

"What are you thinking about?" It's Susan.

"Nothing, really, I swear it." I sound loony.

"Darling, please," she says, embracing me in a way that doesn't make me uncomfortable. "Don't you know you can tell me anything? *Anything?*"

"Anything? I'll tell you everything. Doctor decidedly pessimistic about health issues. Death on the horizon. *Bonne chance.*"

I explain to her, not very adequately, how badly I need their friendship, their discord, their heterosexual theater. Every time I mention Bill she winces.

"It's a little bit crazy you caring about our stupid marriage. After all, it's you and me who are friends from forever; Bill comes so much later. You're my primary relationship."

In college, in Let's Read Everything by Shakespeare class, Susan wrote about Romeo and Juliet. Oh gawd, I thought, not those two tots again. I wrote about Cleopatra. My paper was called "Tragic Love as Hallucinogen." Her paper got an A plus, mine a mere A. But worse, the professor insisted on sending her paper to some erudite journal of Shakespearean thought for publication.

For a lark and the money, we both enjoyed posing nude for the school art class. A life-drawing class. Often we posed together, bodies touching. The issue of inconvenient erection never arose.

While Susan was growing up in a one-parent household she was able to observe a woman, her mother, who had an active political life—not running for office or anything (she was too stylish for that) but supporting worthwhile women and the occasional man. Her mother had a sharp eye and accrued handsome but chilly art that, as soon as the art market enlivens, will do brilliantly at auction.

She has kept her figure, her mother. She sees men now and then but devotes the majority of her affections to a female friend of giantess proportions. The bored speculate they are lovers, but they are not.

Susan's father lives in Hawaii. From the main island he has conducted highly successful business deals (although currently he is resting, waiting for the stock market to enliven . . .). His lady friends are tourists.

"I see—I'm just supposed to pretend everything's okay and whine to you about my disappointing marriage?"

"What choice have we got?"

"You know, they might find something."

"Pretty suede slippers."

"What?"

"Yours, the ones you're wearing."

"You take them."

"If only they would fit, Susan—if only they would fit. Even for a day."

She begins to whimper a bit. "I'll do anything you want me to do, say whatever you want me to say."

"Say nothing, then. Right up to the last second, to say nothing will be the greatest mercy. It will be a way of tricking death out of his artistry. We will embrace the god of marriage instead. Why not? All things smacking of the arbitrary, your marriage, Susan, is the equivalent. The resuscitation of love is a worthy adventure. After all, I didn't get this disease by transfusion. Eros must be obeyed; one can't change lanes so late in the trip."

"But you're still going to go to your doctor and take all your medications, aren't you?" she implores.

"Probably."

I review the alphabet soup of my medications. It is a lure to test Susan, but she has, out of love, absorbed the message. She says:

"We were quiet, but you probably heard Bill and me the other night. Decadent, I know, to kiss lips you no longer trust. But in a city on fire it's necessary to eat, sleep, and touch very fast. If my father hadn't been such an adulterer, perhaps the novelty of betrayal would have interested me. I associated my mother's adulteries with her sophistication. You love Bill, don't you? You see past his shortcomings. Why does life have to be such a Filene's basement when you want it to be House of Dior?"

No doubt very few people understand the purely subjective nature of the phenomenon that we call love, or how it creates, so to speak, a supplementary person, distinct from the person most of whose constituted elements are derived from ourselves.

PROUST

——

Island of Quick Returns

Weather still freezing, we fly away to an island. You might think of this island as a composite of various Caribbean islands, but it really is Nevis.

Our hotel, though new, is a tribute to colonialist tastes. We have adjoining rooms. My room is light pink with terrace doors opening to wildly blowing palm trees and thatched huts artistically arranged near the beach. Black women roast hamburgers under the thatched roofs; one white woman next to them doles out crabmeat. Toasted buns. A tape recorder provides hip-swaying music to which the women are obliged to shift their weight from one leg to the other.

The beach is littered with lovers. Young lovers, middle-aged lovers, old lovers.

Why say "littered"? It's beautiful to fall in love. If couples come for a four-day getaway or week-long honeymoon, hurray for them. I must shed my negativity like a snakeskin on the beach. Look how bright the sun is!

Think Susan and Bill are back together? No; sharing the same room, yes. Fucking furiously morning, afternoon, and nighttime, yes. They, like many, have entered the cadaverous world of Pretend.

I'm expected not to mention that they've never made up, discussed their problems, or even called a truce. That night after the dinner party was just a start to an extended charade of sex and small talk. The hotel waiters seem to get the whole picture. The service is good at the hotel, the men being better servants, the women more sullen.

On the beach, among the nearly naked, I must wear a pajamalike cover-up, freaky angel in a Christmas pageant. Bill is jogging back and forth like someone winning an invisible Ping-Pong game. He's pleased to be able to wear so little among both genders. I see Susan's eyes narrow and narrow some more under her tortoise sunglasses. No woman looks better. Younger ones acknowledge her superb shape with nearly imperceptible tilts of their heads. Susan is regarding the Love Factor. Is it really there somewhere on the hot beach or in the cool water? The fluorescent fish live there; they must have an opinion.

A young girl comes up to us and says to Susan: "I love your skin color—I can't help but ask what lotion you're using. Do you mind?"

Susan says, fiddling through her straw bag, "Chanel. Here, you take it. Listen, I've been observing you and your boyfriend. You're a very attractive couple. I wondered, are you very much in love?"

"What?"

"Are you in love?"

The girl looks electrocuted. "Yes. We're on our honeymoon!"

"Fine. I was only asking. Really, you take this one, I'm going to switch to Coppertone."

The girl disappears like a little girl from the dark cave of a witch. The dark cave remains. When you're unhappy you carry your dark cave around.

I feel so sorry for Susan; even though she's nasty and spoiled, why shouldn't she have joy?

"Was I too mean to that little girl?"

"She got on your nerves."

"Hmm. What lotion are you using?"

I show her; it's identical to the one she just gave away.

"Jesus Christ," Susan says, splitting a Dentyne so we each have a minuscule pink bit to chew on.

Bill, sweaty, pointing at the thatched huts: "Crab or hamburger?"

I'm carrying a note stuck in my underpants.

A letter. It's from the Apollonian, the vibrant Mr. Drake. It reads:

Dear Hector:

I hope you won't think it presumptuous of me writing to you, our social contact being so brief.

I felt terrible the Ded dinner party turned into such a disaster!

Moreover, I wanted to say how much I was enjoying our rapport and felt it a pity it was spoiled by the sudden outburst concerning my engagement.

I want to discuss that with you a little in this letter.

I know that every gay man assumes when another gay man marries a woman there is an implicit deception. I want to be very frank with you, Hector, and say there is no masquerade involved. My fiancée is completely cognizant of the situation. Like you I am HIV-positive, but Jean and I do practice protected sex. As we very much want the pleasure of having a child, we are overjoyed to have found a doctor who has successfully separated the HIV virus from my sperm, which can easily be infused in Jean. She says she is very fertile. We love each other very much.

What do I mean "we love each other very much"? I mean it is easy to sit together for long periods of time undisturbed, peaceful, serene. This cannot be said for most people; think only of the dinner party, where chaotic emotions erupted so readily.

Susan and Bill each mentioned individually how ill you were. I feel very bad for you. Although I too am infected, my T-cell count remains very high and I've had no symptoms of any kind and I'm, for now, relaxed and easy about the condition. I'm certain something will come down the pike to help everyone. Perhaps that's why I've dared to write to you.

When I was growing up, my father died slowly of a particularly vicious cancer. My brothers, sister, mother, and I were forced to tiptoe around, always dreading the next sound of moaning from my father. The fear engendered, eventually, a kind of callousness in all of us, and when my father finally died we were all relieved—no, glad.

Ever since that grim childhood I have sworn off a life governed by fear. I *would* rather be dead. I could not help but notice, at dinner, behind all your wit and sparkle, the specter of Fear.

Forgive me, please, for the intimacy of these observations, but they are intended to alert and perhaps soothe. They are out of love intended. Have a beautiful life, long or short. I must seem a little farcical waltzing in like a superhero—yes, I'm fully aware of the absurdity of my good looks but, gratefully, they'll be lost one day and I'll be relieved—no, glad!

Love,
Maxwell Drake

P.S. I didn't know if your last name was spelled
Diaz or Dias so I made the *z* look like an *s* or the
s look like a *z*. I hate when I get mail addressed
Drake Maxwell—!

A letter. Hardly erotic that I should keep
it tucked in my underpants. But I can't stop reading it.

When it first arrived I was numbed by the surprise of it. I only found it because I went back to my
apartment to get my suitcase and pack a few summer things for the trip. The letter in the box was
crowded by the usual junk, creditors screeching. I
read it standing up over the sink, the faucet dripping. So perplexed by its message I began to count
the number of "I"s in the text: "I hope . . . I felt . . .
I want . . . I know." Then I went after his bride's
name, Jean. Jean Machine. Dream Genie. Jeanne
d'Arc, Norma Jean, Jean Brodie.

"What does any of this have to do with me?" I
asked the sink.

I took in the room. Oldish movie posters. *Le
Mépris, Querelle.* A bit collegelike, not really fit for
someone *older.* Anyway, the room knows I abandon
it routinely now. I tell it where I'm going and how
it won't be so cold there.

In the airport, waiting for Susan and Bill (their
car service is unreliable, they explain later), I open
and close the letter like one of those paper fortune-
teller props girls constructed in grade school to pre-
dict the color of their grooms' hair. By the time I

was on the plane I was able to decipher some of the principles of the missive. Yes, it had the scent of kindness. But a second or third perfume had been mixed in; I couldn't name it, but it made me dizzy, so I finished my fizzy water and went to the toilet booth. Miraculously, there was no line.

Seated inside the minuscule bathroom, where all the little soaps, mini-moisturizers, razors, and petite paper products await their defilement, I reread the letter. Now I really didn't know what it was saying. Did it say "I want to marry you"? Or that he had cancer and that his nurse team had discovered a way to separate the HIV virus from the blood-stream as well as the bone marrow? A woman named Jean: Jean would be the godmother of our child, and . . .

The creature in the mirror (the one I told you about with the funny laugh) speaks now. "Hey, *Wacky*, face the music—it's over! Finished! Do you know what 'finished' means? It means *finished*."

I recollect a bunch of Jean Rhys novels I pigged out on during an unfortunate and extended period of needing to identify with dejected, crumbling characters. Anyhow, these types would always be having a *fine*. What was that? An after-dinner drink? I guess so. "I'll have a *fine*," I said, flushing the toilet.

They were pounding on the door now, the stewards and the stewardesses. They must have heard my pounding on the mirror. It doesn't break. Designed, I suppose, so even if you crash in the Himalayas you can still admire yourself.

Bill and Susan are outside the slender door, among the uniformed. Something has been said about me, and a lot of sympathy begins.

I promise Bill and Susan, in a whisper voice, not to "act up" anymore on the trip. I'll be good, I say, hiding the letter, a wrinkled skin graft. After all, Bill's paid my ticket, hotel, etc.; it wouldn't be very cordial to die now. Pay or play, they say somewhere.

At the hotel dining room, I always arrive a little early or a little late. I don't want the three of us to be mistaken for some ménage. I do it as a courtesy to Bill. Also, I like my entrance, though my dinner jacket's too plain to compete with Susan's décolletage.

Tonight I have forgotten the letter. It's in a little heap next to the snow cone of Arm & Hammer baking soda that spilled. Someone told me it's the best deodorant, but it doesn't smell like anything.

The other diners are all new. Must be a turnover time: back to the grind, honeymoon over. I tell four different waiters I'll wait to order when the rest of my party arrives. Nothing to drink, thank you.

And then something very shocking happens.

All the faces in the dining room—the diners coupled in twos, some cheerful tables for four—everyone is suddenly changed. Old "lovers" of mine, regrouped with a taste for satire: the timid one with the ruffian, the ambitious one with the professional loser, the sex fiend with the ambivalent one. It's a little party, many long dead. And I'm getting "little looks" from them. Flirtations.

There's Jimi Jimi, who by day worked in a store

selling outlandish, up-to-the-second clothing, and at night performed in dark nightclubs as some kind of composite fright figure culled from television.

At the next table is Warren Long, who when I invited him over for dinner during a blizzard, arrived late but with a big ice cream cake with my name on it!

And the one who insisted I accompany him all the way out to East Hampton so he could collect the mail of his recent ex-lover and throw it away.

And the others.

I hadn't noticed Bill and Susan sitting down, ordering drinks.

"Why is he looking like that?"

"Hector, is anything wrong? What are you staring at? What do you see?"

I finally answer, "People I used to sleep with."

"Yes? Where? I don't recognize anyone," she says eagerly.

"But they are here," I respond.

After the soup and the long period of ordering, I assume the ghosts will evaporate.

But they don't. Loud remarks from a few of them. I rise up out of my seat, dinner napkin falling, squeak of chair, canary yellow cane on the walls and ceiling.

I'd never had a "seizure" before. But, taking two steps, I crumble to the floor and only become conscious again in the island hospital on a stretcher moving toward a spare bed.

The nurses and the doctors were exceptionally

good-looking, as if the building, or this floor at least, were being used as a modeling agency. Treatment, because of the lack of technological equipment, was reduced to my being asked to count backwards by sixes from sixty (sixty, fifty-four, forty-eight).

They did, though, have a particular procedure they pushed: the spinal tap. When planning a trip, the masochistic tourist should take into account the enthusiasm with which the spinal tap is conducted in the freezingly air-conditioned tropical hospital. Almost the entire staff converges for the minor horror.

The day before, for an asking price of fifty dollars, I took a chance with the fortune-teller in the lobby. Surrounded by mangy tropical flowers, her very presence didn't seem like a good omen. Tarot, astrology, palmistry, psychic straight talk, she was there for your choice.

"Will my friends Susan and Bill get back together?" I ask the fortune-teller.

"They are together."

"But not in love. Just pretending."

"Maybe not. Maybe you only think so." A fortune-teller saying "maybe"?

And then I ask about me. "What about my future?"

She looks down at her menagerie of equipment: cards, crystals, crooked candle. She looks up; she looks down again.

What happens then is one of those trippy moments that occur periodically in life: the present picks up on some bit of movie dialogue from the past and delivers it more or less verbatim back at you.

"You have no future."

It's Marlene Dietrich as a gypsy in *Touch of Evil* talking to Orson Welles. He's a big bad sheriff and she's a jaded fortune-teller. It's near the end of the movie.

"You have no future left."

I think I'm remembering it correctly. A cold chill passes through me, but it could just be the MAI, which likes to give chills with fevers.

I give her a hundred-dollar bill and, not wishing to too soon relinquish old movie dialogue, I say, "Keep the change."

After the seizure incident and our return to the United States, travel is permanently removed from any agenda of future possibilities.

We all have some version of a tan. Bill is the darkest. He keeps showing his tan line.

First Voice   Virginity O
my virginity!
Where will you go when I lose you?

Second Voice I'm off to a place I
shall never come back
from
              Dear Bride!
I shall never come back to you
Never!

                            SAPPHO

———

Flesh Off the Bone

In the weeks that follow, my action is to avoid mirrors. Bill, Susan, and I embark on a hunt for spiritual uplifters. These are not underwear attachments but persons, mostly women, who speak at indoor public places with material no worse for being collected from wiser, older texts, thoughts from mortal history, both the pride and the anathema of civilization.

One woman I liked a lot spoke in the simplest

terms but with the most hypnotic, velvety voice. "Love yourself, love yourself" was her lovely motto. Address yourself in the mirror with this love; find ways during the day to express this love; treat yourself as someone you *really* like a lot, as someone you loved. Her fans, and their number was tremendous, would bring her yellow roses. As her wealth grew formidable, her voice remained soothing.

The second spiritual lady had an Indian name and an accent put together from several diverse residences strewn around the world. Infected with the virus herself, she lectured on how metitation could put the virus to sleep. We liked her too, but grew uncomfortable when her partner, with a similarly adopted Indian name, requested we address all checks to Arvin Bukowski. Bill thought it the funniest thing in the world.

Third is one who has even topped the former two in notoriety with her best-seller, *Love*. Her major argument is that the body doesn't exist. Despite this insistence, her body, insofar as it was revealed under stylish clothes, was excellent. She has other ideas too: for example, that the chair you are sitting on doesn't exist, either. These notions, which I don't entirely reject, are picked from a huge, navy-blue Bible-like volume which, as legend has it, was dictated by one psychotherapist to another while in trance.

The body doesn't exist. Well, the more I checked myself out, the truer it seemed. Wasting syndrome. Malnutrition syndrome. I never liked skinny bodies, but mine was becoming downright bony. Susan says people "kill" to lose weight. Susan says clothes hang better on thin silhouettes. She says a fat ass is a sign of moral decrepitude. She says dieting is the only true religion in the United States. She nearly said she thought I should be thankful.

The body doesn't exist. Well, it used to. A painter of considerable success followed me around the locker room of a gymnasium, openly begging for me to pose for one of his paintings. I was swimming daily and weight-lifting at the time and, as a result, did, more or less, look worth begging for. I consented, appeared at the studio, and after some lifeless little drawing he attacked me without impediment, nuzzling ravenously every nook of my body. This could be called worship under the most secular of headings. I yielded for the sake of sensation, vanity, and sheer entertainment.

They say the body is the source of all earthly suffering; in this case, at least, I wasn't the one suffering. I took home the little drawing, which made me look like a convict, and stuck it in a drawer.

Coming out of the bathtub (wild fern scent today), I cannot avoid the full-length mirror. It's there.

Funny how gaunt you can get.

The cable on my TV seems hooked up specifically to some World War II showcase. It doesn't matter what time I turn it on, midday when I can't nap or midnight when I can't sleep, the setting is always the Warsaw ghetto and its subsequent "work camps," quickly revealed by the footage as places of extermination. A clever man escapes and hides in a train car returning with all the valuables of the doomed. He jumps off the train in Warsaw and runs through the soon-to-be-vanished streets, shouting the truth about the camps. But no one will believe him. No one. It's too unbelievable. In America, a woman approaches people on line at the cinema. She shouts the same message: "People are being systematically exterminated in Germany and you're in line for the cinema!" Someone comments! to a companion, "She's crazy."

The relentless footage of carnage includes an unflinching eyeful of what has been called the pornography of horror: testicles, breasts, heaps of nudes devastated by torture and starvation.

This morning on the street I met a contemporary I hadn't seen in a long time. In a mournful tone she said, "I feel so *sad*, you look so *bad*."

She'd been an aspiring poet in college when she and I engaged in my one heterosexual affair. She was a zealous sprite at the time and, although it was certainly only an excursion into that territory, I enjoyed it. Time came and anorexia nervosa and full-fledged nervous breakdown. The next time I saw her she'd become, it seemed by some evil magic, an old woman. She looked really bad.

My cattier friends said, "You slept with *her?*"

Giving up poetry (her ruin), she became (guess what?) a therapist.

"It must be because of her great *tact*," Susan said. Susan was dubbed a "shrink assassin" by one of the dozen or so psychiatrists she told *exactly*-what-she-thought-of-them. Mum or loquacious, they didn't much like it. She would rip up her enormous checks for treatment. Her exit line was always, "I'm okay, you're not."

Susan doesn't really understand what it's like to get old so early and so quick.

Old people do understand. The fatigue, the aching, the thinning away, and the nearly visible retreating of existence. A scarecrow in the waiting room said to me, "It's pretty awful when you remember you were awfully pretty."

Bored of the spiritual advisors, Susan says I need to snack. But since we always end up soaking cucumber strips in rice vinegar, weight gain doesn't come easily.

My doctor prescribes a canned nutritional supplement of the color brown. It's a wallpaper glue masquerading as a chocolate milk shake. I merely have to approach the can, a room away, to begin dry-heaving.

"Well, then, perhaps it's time to begin a treatment of an *intravenously* administered nutritional supplement," says Herr Doktor. "Ten hours through the night."

"I don't think so."

"It saves lives."

"You don't say."

This doctor doesn't really cotton to me. I think the chill started when one day he decided to check my scrotum for lumps—I guess a kind of male version of the regimental mammary check.

He shut off all the lights, the better to crouch down with his flashlight and make his examination.

I don't mind telling you I got an enormous erection, and the pendulous thing swung in his gay face recklessly. I'll never forget his expression, looking up as if I'd done the most inappropriate thing in the world. I still don't see what the big deal was.

Listen, I don't know if I'm giving up on Bill and Susan. I mean this love-fixation thing. Maybe I'm just being a meddlesome nut. I'd even considered matchmaking them both to two different people so they would see how right they are for each other. Clearly it was too late for that, Bill having match-made himself to half of Manhattan.

"You're lonely. Very lonely," the pricey fortune-teller on the island said.

"Introduce me to someone who isn't," I said.

The hotel dining room with the undead still haunts me.

Bill says, "If I could give you half my T-cells, I would!"

He's not a bad lout. But now that I've been to his support group he can't resist continuing to tell me episodes of his sexual compulsion. He flicks his hips a little when he gets explicit.

I've become so desexed by my disease I don't know what he expects me to say. His racquetball partner told him not to confide in me, that gays satirize straight people in their spare time.

I've often tried to figure out what Bill does. He's explained it eleven times, something about rotating money around in a circle, but it's over my head. Spending cash doesn't seem to be a problem, but I've refused all offers of loans.

I think Susan is addicted to Bill. She won't admit it. Not all love stories can end this way. Skinny love is even worse than a skinny body.

They probably wish they had stayed on the island with the hamburger huts and nightclubs with torches of fire. I took some of the pink towels from the room and use them now, mummy-style, to wrap my chest and back before sleep. It's for the sweats. It's terribly inconvenient to get up out of bed and change sleep garments in the middle of the night. Susan says the sweats are "detoxifying," like facials, defoliation, diets, enemas. . . .

I can't blame Bill and Susan too much. They've promised to be with me at the end when really all the flesh is off the bone and I'm a skeleton hooked up to a lot of make-believe-advanced machinery. I've made them swear they will pull the plugs.

"Swear!" I demanded.

Bill swore immediately. "I *will*, even if I go to jail for it, I will." (I love him.)

Susan, stricken; it never occurred to her it would ever come to that. An impossibility. A divorce from reason. Susan is my truer love, because she hates me for asking her and I love her for that.

"*Swear!*" I say.

Susan says, like a hundred different characters whose dark destinies flash through my mind, "*I swear.*"

> The Lord is at hand to save me; so let us sound the music of our praises all our life long in the house of the Lord.
>
> ISAIAH 38

———

Full-Time Help

They bought the house Bill had his eye on. I don't remember them ever discussing it.

Although many associates said it was unclever, Bill paid in cash outright. He enjoyed the rush of that kind of spending. Susan mildly argued they'd have less money to fix up the house, but, in actuality, nothing seemed to impede the house in its rush toward beauty.

I had my own room. A room sad and funny. Old wallpaper with fire engines, ladders, and giraffes with firemen hats. The house was old. Though it had been thoroughly cleaned before we entered, sad little notebooks charting milk production sat on each night table; written in pale pencil, they suggested this property had been part of a dairy farm. Sectioned off now, the barn where the cows probably lived housed a gay couple with their Peruvian-purchased baby. Other buildings, including an ice house, were sublet as country retreats.

"I don't know what to keep. I do not know what to keep," said Susan.

Nearly every object in the house had a tag Scotch-taped to it with someone's name on it. Bobby, Davey, Iris, Lila, Montgomery, Lucy, Thomas, Philip, Diana, Petey, Caris, and Denise. The old man had gone to the trouble of selecting the various antiques in his home to go to particular children and grandchildren. It is practically unbelievable that this mob, out of some newfound hatred for their father and grandfather, decided to forfeit all the fine English and American antiques and up the price of the house, as one horrid and nearly elderly grandchild said, "with all the junk in it."

To an amateur eye accustomed only to driveway tag sales, this was a dazzling array of goods: pewter candlesticks; flecked mirrors framed with gold wreaths and eagles; tables of deep red mahogany, tables of honey-drenched maple, tables of delicately flaking paint, green and blue; chairs of cane; spool beds; fourposters; European divans; eccentric china; utilitarian sterling; porcelain birds with their prey; a teacup collection to rival the Smithsonian's; rugs; mammoth bureaus with cut-glass knobs; ticking clocks; chests full of tablecloths and embroidered dinner napkins; kerosene lamps; mono-grammed sheets; costume jewelry; marbles; playing cards; old toys; books; ancient magazines; framed reproductions; crumbling paper dolls; copper pans; neckties; and witty potholders.

Mag came over, the editor with the self-explanatory name. She wanted to do a before-and-after feature in the style section. She was opposed to Susan getting rid of anything. "If you get rid of even one of these hook rugs I'll call you insane. In print." For once she resisted asking me if I wanted a before-and-after feature done on me. I suppose I was too far *after* to be worth the gloss. Her quiet husband came along. He went for a walk alone, os-tensibly to survey the property. She frowned as if there were something decidedly effeminate about such an action.

"And I know just who should re-cover your couches. Let me just photograph this darling little teacup collection. I'm not saying what I'm going to do with it, but one roll of film never killed anyone."

There seemed an easy, dark poetry everywhere lately . . . the editor's tips, the still-bare winter trees outdoors even though spring had already made its moves on Manhattan. I could open any drawer and find old baseball cards, a Bakelite bracelet, or stubs from a show long closed. Or I could go outside to the nearby brook, where last year's leaves moved dead over one another. That's detachment, I told myself. The little war of chirping birds—that at-taches you again. Bill pointed out where rose bushes would be planted. "Not enough sun," Mag

said. "Chop down some trees," she added, embold-
ened by the brisk outdoors.

Abandoned by so many relatives, the house
mourned what it guessed would be an invasion of
Italian wicker furniture, steel plant stands, and
blown glass light fixtures. Americana would lose.

"One hooked rug missing, Susan, and your
name is mud."

"Pick one out you like and take it."

Mag snatched up the one she'd been on the floor
caressing, rolled it up, and stuck it in her convertible before any minds could be changed.

I brought some of my own things to the house,
but they were put in boxes in the basement. Did
I really need to see old notebooks, journals of
crushed crushes, descriptions of flower arrange-
ments and mad seating plans, repetitive memos,
telephone numbers, reportage on disorienting holi-
days, elaborate trips to visit near-strangers? All of
it tied up in the basement with cow memorabilia.
Other things from my apartment I just gave up. A
poor person in my building took most of the furniture. She didn't seem grateful, charity having long
since become a kind of nuisance for her and her
starving children.

The landlord promised me six thousand dollars
to move out. After receiving the keys he declared
bankruptcy. The Deds said not to worry.

I don't worry, not really. Nights and at feeding
times I can hardly breathe. When I wake and stand
up my feet are pins and needles. Neuropathy. Living in the country, I've abandoned all the friends

who've abandoned me. The telephone, for the first time in its long life, has become a shy child. On the other hand, the clock and the wristwatch have become my commandants: pills, infusions, and sharp injections for every twitch of their ticks.

"Time for your shot, darling."

Susan was not squeamish about needles. She sits on the bed with me and we pretend to be East Village junkies.

"Tell me what you thought about what Maggie said," Susan said, depositing my used needle in the red rubber biohazard-wastes dispenser (SHARPS).

"I thought what she said was pretty obvious: save everything, sell everything, throw away everything. The hooked rug scene was touching. Her husband seems more batty. She does too."

"She said I should gut the extension the caretaker lived in with his extended family."

When we had all come for the closing of the house, the white-trash family was still living in this freak arm of the house, which was done up trailer-park-style, replete with cereal boxes everywhere you looked. The cereal family had been there for some time as the old man owner disintegrated, and then, after his death, the owner's children just couldn't be bothered sacking the brood. Bill paid them, pawning them off on a fellow philanderer, a big-wheel lawyer who had just bought an estate in Montauk.

To personalize my room a bit, I placed various bric-a-brac I'd collected on my own, endearing me-

mentos of a good shopping eye. I kept my needles in a great big jelly jar, for everyone to see.

Bill would come back and forth from work, an hour-and-ten-minute drive "door to door," he would say.

Susan and I spent a lot of time together. That's not true; a lot of time was spent with a variety of work people: the carpenters who would gut, the plumbers who would explore, the restorers who would warn, the modernists who would sell, the landscape artists who would overcharge. Neither Susan's nor Bill's parents came to witness the spending fiesta—an act of rebellion, in both directions. Other couples, at least, were willing to spend the whole of Saturday stripping the pre-Roosevelt paint from the window frames. Bill and Susan could not have their icy terrain challenged by spackle. It was more agreeable to agree on everything. It was more agreeable to focus on me.

"Bill, we have to *do* something for Hector. He has malabsorption syndrome or whatever it's called and has to eat all day. We need help. Full-time help."

"A youth from town," Bill ventured. My interest piqued, I leaned over the bannister, eavesdropping.

"Someone who could do a little of everything."

"Especially cook."

"A cleaner who isn't squeamish."

"A presence remote and unobstructive."

"A youth with no ambition. A young drudge happy to have the tax-free dollars. A fine fellow."

Fine fellows did not line up for their interviews. In fact, only one fine fellow appeared at all for the job.

I detest it when old fogies remark jocularly they-can't-tell-if-it's-a-boy-or-a-girl! when confronted with some extravagant hairstyle on an adolescent. But honestly, I could not, for the little life left in me, ascertain the gender of our new houseperson. Kim.

Kim could've been a girl and he could have been a boy. The name itself was open to interpretation, and none of us felt bold enough to just ask, "Which is it?" I decided he was a boy.

Kim made my peanut-butter-and-jelly sandwiches, my cream-cheese-and-jelly sandwiches, my olive-and-cream-cheese sandwiches, and, when Bill and Susan were around, vile steaks. "Au poivre," Kim said as we choked and swore.

Kim changed my sheets. Kim did my bathroom. Very clean for a disheveled creature. He mentioned saving for college, but I don't believe even high school was a fait accompli.

I never grew fond of Kim as I ought to have. He cried only once, and bitterly, when all traces of the white caretakers were removed and crushed in dumpsters.

"The refrigerator was new," Kim moaned. "One just had ice cream in it. They both worked. Two."

He was given a sweet little room off the kitchen, what perhaps was meant as a breakfast room. Lilac-flecked paper, painted floors. It was dear, but he didn't go for it, and when his grief over the gutting didn't abate, he insisted Bill drive him some distance to a down-and-out dance hall so he could "let out some steam."

The biggest problem was his phone manner. He had a fugitive's curtness, a xenophobe's fear of an unfamiliar voice. A hanger-up. It infuriated Bill.

"She's not full-time help—she's a full-time pain in the house!" He'd missed a moneymaking call. He craved spaghetti. Kim couldn't make spaghetti.

"Bill, he's reliable. He's always here. In case of an accident, he's always here," Susan said.

"He can't drive!"

"He's learning, Bill. Think of the ones we've had in New York. They swear loyalty and vanish like informers. Argentina, Chile, Guatemala, Zaire, Ecuador, Provence—what foreign port haven't they flown to? Sometimes without even a phone call, most swearing up and down they will be back. Things missing from our drawers. Surly conversations in front of our faces in unknowable tongues. Shady friends with unclean clothes manning the kitchen. Drunks!"

"Calm down, Susan—you're not PC enough to take this diatribe out of earshot. True, Kim sleeps here, but what other options does he have? Limitless, I guess, since he's a hermaphrodite."

"Well, he makes the bed beautifully. You remember Diana, who would always leave the inner pillow cover with the zippers exposed when one hundred times we said the zipper goes on the inside?!"

"But the food!"

"The tuna salad was no worse than at the Quilted Giraffe. Better. More onions. Don't forget we're doing it all for Hector and *he* hasn't complained. Kim helps him up and down the stairs. He said if the event came, he'd be willing to change his diapers. Kim has problems—he can't read or write, vacillates on the subject whether his parents are dead or alive—but goddammit, he's *there*."

I didn't know they had tuna salad at the Quilted Giraffe. Kim put curry in the egg salad; I told him to. He doesn't mind me having AIDS and never mentions God's point of view in relation to it.

"The hospital is a short drive away," Susan says biweekly. I don't comply with the wishes of those who enjoy a short drive. Every two weeks I go with Bill back into the Big Town and I acquire more exorbitantly priced drugs, fresh needles for my jelly jar, and bath products. Eucalyptus, Lavender, Sandalwood, Orange, Vetiver, Pine, Fern, Cedar, Rosemary, Rosewood, Tuberose, and a plethora of Dead Sea Salts. Except for the American Cedar scent, all others sport Italian tags proclaiming, *"miracolo— fantastico . . . ,"* and then in English, "reviving."

When I'm on Manhattan Island I'm always struck (like everyone else) by the variety. The burn victims in Courrèges. Pansies with Pekinese or in window boxes. Puerto Ricans with husky pound dogs. Negroes with white pussycats. Knife-wielding children; infants pleasantly mismatched to their guardians; Brazilian parrots on the shoulders of mad people (a parrot says desperately, "I'm stuck, Tony—I'm stuck. Tony, help me—help me, Tony. Tony, I'm stuck").

After I collect my medications and new prescriptions, Bill and I go out to lunch. To watch the foxy ladies. Bill's technique has the subtlety of an atomic bomb, but his good looks seem to collect only happy victims. I'm expected not to notice or, alternately, to concur the woman in the tangerine suit would be a juicy candidate to peel.

Bill has the oyster stew and a glass of cold wine. Thinking of my spiritual development, I have the almond sole. It comes with a boiled potato. Philanderers from his club wave to Bill from their indiscreet tables. The waiter, who looks like an exhausted entrepreneur, baggy-eyed and messed-up, says, "Have the coconut custard." I order it because I figure he must know something I don't. "Custard pudding is going to make you very happy." Think of that. When the custard arrives, I'm half-believing I'll remove a hypo and inject the dessert. But could a cure for unhappiness cost only six dollars?

After the lunch Bill drives to the station. I'm not on the train long, and Susan is waiting in her convertible for me. It's five o'clock now, so we might be a Cheever story. Kisses on the cheeks. The Bain d'Hadrian is delivered.

Susan takes it up to one of the many claw-footed bathtubs. She grabs also her waterlogged *Anna Karenina*. Susan says she's rereading everything worthwhile. "It shouldn't take long." We're doing remedial Tolstoy. I'm reading *Resurrection;* Bill, the *Wall Street Journal*.

Kim appears, mumbling about the marketing. I don't have another pill procedure for several hours, so I volunteer to accompany him. We hop in his truck (he or she could easily be as young as fifteen) and he drives like a demon on fire. New driver, no license.

The market, predictably, is a gargantuan ice palace. Freezing lanes of "vacuum-packed" goods. There's even a little kit to vacuum-pack at home. The food hall is curiously empty. The majority of people are found buzzing around the insecticides, garden tools raised.

We collect canned goods: crushed tomatoes, pitted olives, the usual essentials. Frostbite from holding dead meat in cellophane. Fish like socks. Lettuce. "Health" dressings you see so often on television you feel you must have them. Ranch. Closed-circuit television lets you watch a little black-and-white version of you vacillating. From the overhead lights a general glow ignites both the labels and the people, and although everything is more or less presentable, it all seems supranatural and unsellable.

I don't know why, but I suddenly experience a premetaphysical rush. Hot and cold tingling. Maybe it's because I'm holding a can of white asparagus tips, which reminds me of what they were serving in the dining room of the Hotel of Seizures.

Maybe it's the vision from the adjoining Laundromat, a woman jumping and gyrating in a frenzy fit to revive the old Studio 54. Her dance, in temple pajamas and running shoes, amply supplies a clue (accompanied by an electrical buzz and distant Muzak—the omnipresent and telling "Raindrops Keep Falling on My Head") to twenty-first-century shopping. I happen to know for a fact the robots replacing the cash-register clerks will be arriving any day now.

Anyway, taking all this into account, I turned and asked Kim, "Where is God?"

You must have faith in what I'm going to tell you next.

Kim let out a high-pitched screech, a surreal wail, a cry I haven't heard anywhere outside the Bronx Zoo.

Our religious discussion aborted by this primal sound, we headed back to the truck. I thought I'd approached the subject too head-on. I countered with small talk: admiration for frozen peas, encouraging remarks on his driving.

There must be more to Kim, this little sexless creature in the wild. But even secular probing led nowhere.

One morning an intravenous apparatus appeared, a hookup for a ten-hour nightly nutritional supplement. "Until you make up for lost pounds!" said the doctor. Kim would come into my room with a flashlight more than once in the night, checking to see the drip was going well. He was an interesting little nurse. I wondered if he had access to a pistol. For me, of course, if it came to that.

Like the last blood transfusion, the IV of nutrition seemed to help a bit, and I had more energy to survey the land, the ponds, the brooks, the alleys of fine fir trees.

Nature, to itself, never seemed sufficiently lonely. Already the insects and plant seeds were flying everywhere. Rocks with lichen were alive with their green face masks. It was like a book party with no place to sit. The book was fabulously illustrated, but there were no explanations for anything. One grew numb to be participating so vividly in a story so indecipherable, the author absent.

I asked if there was a church nearby. I was told there was a seminary, but at first I thought they said "a cemetery." I didn't want to visit the seminary. I imagined half the young priests would be homosexual, ogling each other in spurts of guilt, would eventually drop out or spoil their congregation with news of their naughtiness. There was a military academy nearby too. That would have an entirely different allure, but I didn't even daydream about it. Having consigned myself to neuter status, I could increasingly identify with Kim, who (although I knew he would run away one day) I decided was a good soul.

Maybe that is what one is looking for throughout life, that and nothing more; the greatest misery there is to feel, so as to become oneself truly
before death.

CÉLINE

———

The Disco Inferno

Susan said she might write a novel. She asked me if
I would mind if she wrote about me. "What about
me?" I asked. "You know," she said, "someone
who's ill and . . . not feeling well."

I'm in a clinical trial. The obese Romanian
woman who weighs me and takes my blood is
resigning. She says she's going to work with burn
victims in the burn ward. She assures me the burn
victims will be much easier to work with. You can't
get ahead with AIDS, she says, clarifying.

A woman of color has replaced the Romanian.
Her name is Cassandra, and her inappropriate

smile is prescient as her name. She faxes the blood reports to my cynical doctor. I guess her cynicism to be of a philosophical variety, that she believes after a hideous ordeal comes a transcendental payoff. I compliment her earrings to get her to talk. She's engaged to be married, she says. I can't, for now, get any more out of her. The doctor who fuzzies my eyes with weekly drops, flashing photos and conducting near-kissing examinations nose to nose with sci-fi spyglasses, is just married. He's pleasantly virile and I ask him, very suggestively, how everything is going with his new marriage. My blood goes up, my blood goes down, my blood count goes round and round.

No one uses the word "stable" around me—it would be considered absurd in the surprise party of immune deficiency.

In the middle of the week, coming out of the downtown branch of my blood factory (uptown, midtown, all around the town, on various marked afternoons), I ran into my old friend Noh.

Noh wasn't his real name; it was an adaptation to cover up the fact he'd grown up in a trailer park sandwiched between two military retirees.

He learned several languages, bicycling to the nearest library with earphones and records of the distant tongues, and attained a reading list of the toniest world literature. A moderate beauty with panic and an unkillable determination to make a splash somewhere away from the rural, he ran away to the country's most aggressive city. I don't know how much thorough practice he got of his foreign languages, but I often saw him in the company of people who spoke in thick, affected accents: people on the way to Majorca who'd just left Cairo but might be in Malibu by Christmas if the house is lost in Maui; Paris is still nice, isn't it? I left a pair of suede pants in Pascale's apartment in the Seventh.

I don't know who christened Timmy "Noh," but he said a prostitute named Oui thought of it. A joke? I don't think he ever became the artistic sensation he dreamed about in the library. He did get some notoriety writing and directing (without pay) something Dada and lurid called *The George Washington Menstrual Cycle,* a continuing soap opera played at midnight in a seedy but fashionable nightclub. Other outlandish theater adventures gained some ink in the press, a chance for him to invent and advertise himself as a person whose wide experience and agile tongue derived from parents in "high echelon" government, sprinting around the globe, toting their towhead wunderkind.

"Are you well?" asked Noh.

"Timmy, I'm practically dead," I said, deliberately irritating him with his real name. (He told it to me once, crying in a toilet stall, the Sex Pistols' "Pretty Vacant" playing in the background.)

I liked Noh best when we went dancing. We were dance buddies (no-sex-please-we're-friends). Sometimes he would call four in the morning and say, "Let's go to the Sound Factory!" Okay, I would say.

I went through a very long period of being

agreeable. Unattractive people, unattractive places, unattractive invitations—I seem to recall accepting all of them. I suppose I saw Noh as a mirror image, not lighter or darker, maybe a tad more intellectual. He urged me to read a fourteenth-century German mystic with a hard-to-pronounce name. Meister Eckhart. For someone who went to an awful lot of parties, it was interesting Noh should so surely recommend a man who recommended the principle of renunciation. Eckhart, he said, who was an expert of speculative mysticism, was to be tried by the diocese as a heretic, but he went and died first.

I did like dancing with Noh. The Deds said Noh knew everyone. They were very impressed with all his shiny name-dropping. With enviable timing he sold at auction a homely (seventies) Warhol, days after the beloved cadaver was buried. Other valuable paintings hung within his reach: an inexplicably attained Franz Kline, a messy little Pollock he said he got from going to bed with him—but that would be chronologically impossible, so you see the *faux* of Noh.

The Sound Factory was enchanting, black, industrial, and ugly with taped twittering birds piped into the corridors and bathrooms with the panache of springtime in hell. The dance floor whirled with expert dancers, mostly black; a sizable smattering of exquisite drag queens with the hauteur of dictators; pumped-up white boys shunning love; some girls, a little lost, a little outrageous; and all the other detritus of Fun.

"Oh, there's Tom. He knows all the best hustlers

in L.A. And he's wearing Judy's favorite colors: green and yellow."

The fact of the matter was the dance floor (hot to the touch) provided an arena for erasure, the individual and tribal urge to disappear into some definitive primal gesture. Hiding from death.

Before I got (PCP) pneumonia and nearly died, Noh took me with his "excess miles" to Argentina.

It was an act of lonely generosity and great patience as I coughed and gasped my way into the pampas. Throwing up every meal and walking as fast as a tiny ant, I got it into my head I had to get to the Iguaçu Falls. An American woman in the lobby of our antiquated hotel in Buenos Aires said no one should die without seeing the Iguaçu Falls.

I still haven't seen them.

I'm going to skip over the whole later part of my tube-covered stay in the hospital (a triumph for my doctor). Suffice it to say, on boarding the plane to return, I heard the stewardess whisper to my friend, "Is he going to make it?"

I could never hate Noh. Susan said he stole some money she had out on her dresser, that she didn't care but I should know for my sake.

I told him about living with Bill and Susan. I asked him to lunch, my treat (more and more I felt I had to pick up the tab, to deflect my bad-omen status of being ill).

Over old-lady consommé and room temperature Waldorf salad I told Noh about my little crush on Maxwell Drake, pretty much verbally reproducing the letter he'd sent me.

"What's his name—Maxwell Drake? He used to pose for romance novel covers and was photographed as a fireman in a calendar, although he was no fireman! He's dead. Dropped to the sidewalk, five days in the hospital, clogged lungs, quite dead now. Recently. Oh, asymptomatic people are all very superior until the ax falls."

Did I tell you I clutched little balls of half-used tissues, my talismans? I dipped down to pick up the one that fell.

Did I tell you I called Mr. Drake several times on the telephone? Well, I did, but I never got an answer. I left some stupid, vague messages on the machine.

Dead now too. The vogue.

We ordered another round of iced tea but sat speechless stirring diminishing ice. We'd seen each other naked (not literally, thank God; he was always a pale, skinny thing, long before I lost all my color and looked like a scarecrow), and it made conversation difficult. He was HIV-positive too, or seropositive, or "exposed to the virus," or whatever way one chose to name it.

"I have a terrible headache," I said, touching my forehead. "The pills I take are all in conflict, and I get so dizzy. I told you, didn't I, I'd had a seizure? I was hallucinating at the time too, I think."

Back at the Deds' apartment, Bill was busy moaning up a storm. I went back out and bought a magazine. When I came back in and they were finished, I was introduced to a girl named Shush— and on other occasions, a girl named Sheila and another named Charlotte. Bill introduced all these girlfriends free of self-consciousness. I was invited to dine with them with the same spirit I was invited to the Lowly Husbands Club. I don't know why Susan was wasting her time writing a novel about a corroding invalid when she had a hot property in her philandering husband. I read in the *New York Times* book review section about a woman who made scads of money reproducing her husband's sex diaries, just changing names—say, from Trudy to Tootie or Carmella to Taffy. Noh said it didn't matter what Susan wrote, that she wasn't a "real" writer. Funny, that's what Susan had said about Noh. In college Susan wrote stabbing little poems I rather admired. She could take an angry turn of phrase, dress it up with criticisms of nature, and make it almost Japanese.

I recently read someone's (a Frenchman) account of this disease and his death by the hand of it. I thought the book lacked the joy and humor of deterioration. My doctor said I should seriously consider the use of antidepressants.

Over dinner at the Oyster Bar I told Bill about my meeting with Noh, the news of the sudden death of my nonlover and one-letter correspondent, Maxwell. "Well, that's amazing!" said Bill.

Dinner talk was strained, because Shush kept interrupting, or, more to the point, Bill kept telling her to shut up. I was beginning to see Bill was something of a woman hater, as perhaps all promiscuous men are; and seeing also that Susan was fast becoming a man hater, resenting a man who made her feel loathsome about her situation. Is it any wonder the sexless Kim was fast becoming the most popular member of our household?

I'd tried to encourage Susan in some retaliatory intercourse, suggesting the assistance of a man who came to collect dead leaves with a blow machine. He was very good-looking, considering. But Susan said she was reluctant to get into a sexual tit-for-tat with Bill. She'd rather buy a dildo, she said. What happened to the one she had in college? I asked.

While Shush (an almost pretty woman with an old-fashioned who-me?-what-did-I-say?-where-am-I? kind of shtick) slurped down she-crab soup, I told Bill how well Noh looked, the subtext obviously being that Noh remained AIDS-free, for now.

"Didn't he steal money once from Susan's bureau?" Bill said between mouthfuls of oyster stew, dripping a little.

I had a baked potato and remembered Noh telling me about a mysterious dinner party he'd attended, with minor celebrities (an atonal composer who published diaries about his lost beauty; a movie critic; his one-screenplay-writing girlfriend, a lush with an Oscar, dressed up like a drunken Pierrot; a hostess who'd been in a film noir classic in which she repeatedly threatens to blow up the world; and her troubled but successful music-video-maker son) and culminating in the unsolved theft of everyone's handbags and wallets left unattended on the guest-room bed. Suspicion, I believed, would fall heavily on Noh's head (after all, he was the most certifiably weird member of the party, younger, with contradictory biographical info: high school in Venice, high school in Englewood, high school in Osaka). He was fascinated with all the possibilities (omitting his own ravenous greed and general contempt for the guests), as if it were a game of Clue.

Are you a make-believe person? I wanted to ask Noh.

The whole time growing up I believed you had to collect bits of yourself and Scotch-tape them all together. There were the people who did that expertly and the ones whose tatty handiwork showed on their souls and faces. I hated meeting lonely people, since every encounter was a glaring example of my own longing. Noh seemed to solve this problem by carrying around a mental hate list of all the people he'd perceived as getting in his way to "the top." The only time he mentioned his parents to me was to say they abused him. He said his father used to pull down his pants, put him across his lap, and hit him while his mother, in her bra and jeans, leapt up and down, shouting, "Spank him until he bleeds!"

I hope Noh isn't a liar (or a thief). It would be awful to know even his truth is false. I don't mind so much someone called Timmy renaming himself after Japanese dramas, but it would be a pity to know you'd been sitting around for a decade listening to a lot of bullshit.

Although it's true the Iguaçu Falls never made it into our travels (saving the best for last is a very dangerous venture in this trick-trap world), we did satisfy the demented impulse to fly (using five different airplanes, including—the last—an army one) to the very bottom of Argentina, Tierra del Fuego.

It was freezing and populated by hunters. We'd mistakenly confused this location with perhaps some exotic part of Mexico mentioned in a short story by Jane Bowles or someone like that.

Anyway, sitting with Noh at the Tante Ilvira, a crude but, for the region, highly rated restaurant filled with men and some women wearing red-and-black wool jackets and holding rifles, I cut my finger on my house-special order of giant crab. The blood beaded on my red thumb and Noh, saying nothing at first, took up the white-flecked shell with its claw teeth and sea gloss and punctured his own thumb. "We are now blood brothers," he said, squeezing our two bloody thumbs together.

I'd only recently been diagnosed and hadn't yet been forced into the blood parade of continual testing. Noh picked up my cut thumb and, really surprising me, sucked my blood. It seemed way beyond the call of brotherhood, but I never asked him about it. Maybe we further infected each other. "Everyone's going to get it," he said. "It's a plan, but not by the government as a lot of paranoid people think. *Read Eckhart*," he added ominously. Though I couldn't even spell it, I assured him I'd get right on it.

I want to say more about the disco inferno, but it's difficult conjuring its charm if you haven't heated yourself therein. People hating their parents, jobs, apartments, roommates, spouses, and (in some cases) children; people jumping up and down, twirling.

A lot of Timmy Noh has to do with this predawn dervish; past and future left at the door, the present a sand grain made imperial.

That's not a very good explanation, but it's true. Noh Timmy, unlike me, seems to be in very good health. Noh said he just might take Susan Ded's cue and write a book about all the people he knows dropping dead. Why not? he said; they couldn't sue.

"You should," I said encouragingly.

"Beat Susan to the punch. *You* couldn't do it; it would be a waste of time. You wouldn't be able to enjoy it, to get the laugh out of it. You'd be dead."

"So true," I said, wondering what was Cruelty; the extremity of my situation made truth, reality, practicality, good sense, and even kindness seem like vicious cousins.

Before incinerating a bunch of old journals and mounds of why-did-I-keep-these? papers, I found a Xerox of a letter I once wrote to a paramour in Florida.

Odd that I'd bothered to make a copy of this dashed-off note. I reread it with a sense of meeting a complete stranger. I will present it to you. It proves I have no business describing anyone, least of all myself, clearly a person I could no longer know, whose desires and sentiments have become irrevocably alien:

Dear Phil:

It's sad you have no one to rub dicks with—
why don't you steal something from the house,
sell it, and send me the airfare? I would be glad
then to lend you mine. Just an idea. Pink and
orange decor? Sounds pukey but perhaps
driving around in a Lincoln could be fun:
windows tightly shut, driving way too fast,
parking, covering most of the seats with cum,
not cleaning it off, etc. Everyone is over fifty—
you should do what I do. Bathe with the
door open, lather up your cock, and start
conversations of seeming innocence with
passersby in the hall, squirt. I suppose it is good
for you to have this time to think without
alcohol or drugs. Tell me what you come up
with. Could you print your next missive? You're
hard to read. What was my night like that night?
I passed a phone booth, it rang, I answered it,
they asked about my cock, begged me to come
over, I said as long as you're not bummed out
if I leave abruptly because I turn out to be
uninterested, I went, very interesting. Attractive
blond ravenously devouring my penis for hours
near a portable heater. I enclose photos that I
thought in your solitude might amuse you.
Beach scenes. The guy in the red neckerchief
has your expression on his mouth. I also
thought the three on the rocks sweet. And
anyway when you tire of them I'm sure you can
pass them on to the lady of the house so she
might pin them up in her changing room. She'll
enjoy, I'm sure, the stains you'll supply to the
paper. Your next party you must throw in

another space entirely—darker with fuck nooks,
don't you agree? And you mustn't be so
inhibited in your attire; I suggest you dip your
dick in strawberry jam, making sure to get a lot
on your balls and pubic hair—and that's it,
certainly no socks or shoes. I am so sick of New
York the necropolis (to save you the trip to the
dictionary—that means city of death or death
city) and wish I could go at once to some
languorous address undressed, baby oil, melons,
etc. This past weekend it was seventy-five
degrees and today below freezing. I'm terribly
bored. Many glamorous events fill this week—
I'm not bragging, it's simply true—but I am so
in need of change.

Soul kisses from your personal friend,

Hector

Experience must always be an experience of
something, but disinterest comes so close to zero
that nothing but God is rarefied enough to get
into it, to enter the disinterested heart. That is
why a disinterested person is sensitive to nothing but God.

MEISTER ECKHART

———

Prayer

Kim made lasagna. He browned little bits of cubed
tofu to resemble meat and said it was vegetarian.

Susan, to bone up for her own book, kept rereading the section in Tolstoy where Anna and
Vronsky exile themselves to a country estate so they
can hear less castigation (about their adultery) from
friends and neighbors.

When the telephone rings, Bill jumps up to answer it. It's Shush.

"That's right, you get it, Bill. She hangs up every
time I answer it. Invite her for dinner! We haven't
had any good laughs around here in a while."

Bill comes back in the room and says, "I have. I've invited her for dinner. Tomorrow. Cocktails on the porch at six. Dinner when Kim feels like it. How about it, Kim? Seven, eight, nine—we don't care."

Kim, who's been guarding the door to the kitchen, animates himself excitedly to say, "Cold soup at 7:45. Tofu brochettes at 8:05. Sprout-filled pineapple halves, papaya dressing. Spiked iced tea."

"Splendid," says Bill, suddenly wolfing down his no-meat lasagna, which he'd previously redistributed around his plate like a five-year-old.

Kim is closely examining damp old cuisine magazines with spots all over them, retrieved from the basement. Antique ideas about putting marshmallows in casseroles. Couldn't possibly have all these tofu recipes. Kim's changing into a really confident cook, even if everything he serves, thanks to the ongoing construction in the house, is covered with a white dusting of plaster.

"Any dietary restrictions, your friend? Kosher?" Kim asks considerately.

"Kosher? She's breaking one of the Ten Commandments—what does she care about kosher?!" shouted Susan.

The next day, in the evening, Bill goes to pick up Shush at the train station.

"Shush? That's her name? That's on her birth certificate? What's the rest of it—B. Quiet? How do you know her name? Have you met her?"

"We had a meal together," I say.

"What? Alone?"

"With Bill."

"With Bill! The three of you? That doesn't count as a traitor act to you?"

"No."

"No. No. I agree. I would've gone too. Definitely."

I don't think Susan fully comprehends that Bill will walk in any minute now with this new girlfriend of his. She thinks his betrayal is a general thing with no specific characters.

We hear the sound of Bill's Range Rover over the gravel. I guess Bill just cracked a joke, because Shush enters laughing.

She isn't exactly as I remember her. Less cartoonish, more normal, and therefore more threatening.

Susan says, blocking the hallway, "I'm Mrs. Ded."

"Hello. You can call me Shush. That's my real name."

Bill pushes past Susan and says, "And you remember Hector. Let's all have something good and icy to drink."

Kim has unearthed an elaborate iced-tea set: tray, tall glasses, and twisted swizzle sticks. We are given minuscule linen napkins appliquéd with hearts to grip the cold glasses.

"Kim, please remove yourself from the porch for a little while," Susan says.

"I have to keep to my schedule."

"Get off the porch now! *Now!*" Kim runs away

and Susan continues: "Excuse me for shouting. It's not like me. It's just that Kim is so young—we don't want to expose him to everything. Why, we don't even know if he's reached puberty yet. What do you think?"

"I think she has," says Shush, smiling, apparently able to drop her dizzy routine at a moment's notice.

"Pardon me, Miss Shush, but I really do feel compelled to ask you what you are doing here. I mean, I know you must take my husband for a total jackass, but how could you possibly believe you could march into my new home and insinuate your pushy vagina in my face? Could you not know my syphilitically minded husband has been with hundreds of similarly demoralized women? Ask him. He makes regular confessions at weekly meetings for compulsives. I foolishly believed such oral display might be a substitute for genital obsession—how wrong could I have been?"

Shush asks, "What are these brown, turdlike things on this skewer?"

"Tofu!" Kim screams from the kitchen.

Bill, with an excellent appetite and talking with his mouth full, says, "Susan, Shush and I were talking the other day how fun it might be if we did a three-way. You know, the three of us in bed together. I think it could be really fun. Maybe Hector could video it—it would be fun to look at later."

"I won't help," I surprise myself by saying so quickly.

"Doesn't matter—we can just set up the camera in one position. One long shot. We'd all be on the bed, so it won't be out of focus."

"I don't think your wife likes me," says Shush. She is wearing a bright pink sunsuit and has her knees pressed up against her chest.

"Susan's very hung-up on her parents' ancient marital discord," says Bill. "But I keep telling her there's no correlation between them and us. Her mother's very cold and her father's a real bastard."

As Bill leans over and grabs two of Shush's untouched brochettes, the dining table trembles a bit and Susan, whiter than the falling plaster, throws up.

I thought she might throw up when Bill mentioned her parents, but I didn't actually believe she would throw up, and so much.

A tiny bit splatters on each of us, but Shush is first on her feet, shouting, "I can put up with a lot, but not a puker! I'm getting out of here! Someone take me to the station! Bill, you drive me home!"

Susan has the glazed-over eyes of a dead woman.

"Look, Susan," Bill says, "it's no big deal. You don't have to do anything you don't want to do. Have I ever forced you to do anything? No. Whose idea was it to get this lovely house? It's yours—it's your house, Susan."

"If someone doesn't get me into some mode of transportation on the double, I will start screaming and I won't stop screaming until the fire department comes to put me out."

"Oh, shut up," Bill says, inevitably.

Personally, I just want to escape.

My tolerance for horrendous behavior has shrunk.

I stand up, unable to take much action. Kim is standing too, in the archway into the pantry, with his papaya concoction. He's wearing the Mao suit Susan found for him in a junk shop in lieu of a chef's outfit. Bill mocks the suit, but Susan said it's a hundred times nicer than the Nixon suits he wears to the office. So you see, things are already off before the iced tea comes out.

When the phone rings, I run to it like I'm saving a drowning friend. Over my shoulder, I hear the bickering take on a second wind, stinkier for the regurgitation.

"Hello," I say; grateful for the distraction.

"Hector, it's *me*." It's a friend I never talk to anymore.

"I ran into Noh," he says. "He said you were getting over a nasty little crush on a Drake. A really big one, actually."

"No," I stutter.

"I get it. Something from Tennessee Williamsland, and you used the Deds to *lure* him, right? Very Sebastian. *Suddenly Last Summer!*"

"No, not at all. The very idea! No, on the contrary, Bill and Susan were attempting some matchmaking. It's only that it backfired."

"Doesn't matter. I hear he's dead anyway. Heart condition, Noh said."

"I don't know if that's even true! Was there a memorial service?"

"Don't isolate yourself, Hector. Now more than ever you need to get out and have a good time!"

I need to get rid of a lot of the bad energy from the dining room and to make up for not defending Susan. I talk now for her. I say, "You must be completely cracked, talking to me like that! Where do you expect me to find all this energy to go out and have a good time? Where on earth?!"

"You're resistant to challenge—challenge yourself. You're resistant to change—*change.*"

"Chummy of you to telephone—don't think I don't appreciate it. I can assure you I'm looking a lot better than Noh might have said."

"I saw someone at the Janet Sartin counter and they were working miracles with cover-ups. Don't be afraid to wear makeup. Makeup can be very virile."

"I'll be sure to say you said so. I must really run now—almost time for my bath and I'm in the middle of an unusual dinner party."

"Good. Noh said you were excruciatingly thin."

"And that blender diet you started last summer—any luck with it?"

"I'll let you go. Keep well and lots of love. Don't listen to anyone who says 'terminal'—what do they know anyway?"

I'm not going to even grace the caller of that call with a name.

I go into my room to lie down. The chenille bedspread is out being cleaned and the light blanket is itchy under me.

It's a pity, because the day started so much nicer.

The country air was so clear and pretty, June before it grows too warm. I was able to convince Bill to drive me to the nearest library. He whistled the whole way because he was going to introduce the semivociferous Shush to his wife that night.

I found two volumes by the Meister Eckhart person Noh recommended. One book was just called *Sermons,* and the other had a more winning title, *The Book of Divine Consolation.*

I reach for the two books on my bed. Boy, do I need it now, I say to myself.

Ripped out of *Newsweek* and used as a bookmark by the previous reader, I find an interview with the Nobel-prize-winning nun, Mother Teresa. It goes like this:

Q. What did you do this morning?
A. Pray.
Q. When did you start?
A. Half past four.
Q. And after prayer?
A. We try to pray throughout work by doing it with Jesus, for Jesus, to Jesus. That helps us put our whole heart and soul into doing it. The dying, the crippled, the mentally ill, the

unwanted, the unloved—they are Jesus in disguise.

I know little or nothing about prayer. Somewhere Eckhart goes on about how the very thought to pray is sufficient and will certainly satisfy God, that actual prayer is not necessarily necessary.

Once I was in a bombing at Orly Airport, the shoddier of the two airports outside Paris. You may have seen the front-page coverage in the newspaper, with a giant photo of the smashed glass wall of the airport and the bloodied victims covered with cloth. I believe the terrorists were Turkish women who blew up with their suitcases to spite Armenians, or else Armenian women who blew up to spite Turks. Either way it was a catastrophe, and flights were halted. We the living were led out into the intense heat of midday to stand in the immense parking lot with our suitcases.

I remember people falling to their knees; I thought perhaps it was because of the terrible heat. Then I noticed some of them mumbling and gesturing to themselves, and I realized they must be praying! What prayer was generally composed of, I didn't know. (I imagined in this case it was "Please don't let another bomb go off.") Truly out of sync with the moment, I said, "Who has the courage to go back into that building for a soda?"

My dare was met with incredulity and language barrier. Unperturbed, I donned my most imperious look, the folder of half-baked poems I was working on at the time under my arm. Believing I must be some bomb expert, the French police filed away from me and I officiously crossed the path of shattered glass and splattered blood to the unscathed soda machine.

I had to have an orange soda.

Perhaps this was a form of prayer. I brought some freezing, heavenly sodas back to the melting crowd. Two thirsty people kissed my hand. The police looked at me suspiciously now.

That was so long ago.

Daydreaming, I forget my needle.

I should have taken it before dinner. The doctor says they are miraculous, that if I didn't have them I'd have to have a transfusion every week.

The main floor is quiet and I go to the kitchen to the Sub-Zero refrigerator for my vial.

Sunk in the tub, I load my needle. I have no buttocks left, but I stand up to prick myself there. It's just a sort of wrinkle now, my ass. And the flesh resists the pierce of the needle, body sick of it, body confused and impatient for final goodbyes. I laugh. My bubble bath today is called Bliss. From a local shop, with incense and temple scarves and relaxation tapes . . .

I don't see how Bill and Susan's marriage can survive this last event. There'll be no avoiding it. Susan's mother will insist her own lawyer be consulted immediately. Susan's father will suggest she come to Hawaii to think things over. Susan will say she can't, that she has to take care of a sick friend who can no longer fly.

Assets will be reviewed. House limits set so Bill

must stay permanently away from the house. Reconciliations, on Bill's part, all denied. Re-evaluation time.

I get so tired. I tell myself I won't even need my sleeping pill tonight. I take it away.

Before falling asleep, I remember the day I told Susan about my diagnosis and retiring T-cells, about my death sentence, my curtailed expectancy.

"This is the worst thing that's ever happened to me," says Susan.

Let that which is lost be for God.

SPANISH PROVERB

——

Luck

My father always said I was unlucky. He shouldn't
have said that.

My new psychiatrist says gay babies need an
erotic/romantic relationship with their fathers such
as straight babies have with their mothers, but since
the likelihood of the gay babies getting such pater-
nal affection is slim, they grow up the way they do.

We went to the law office, Susan and I—indeed,
a lawyer friend of Susan's mother's. A cold-blooded
type, this lawyer. I thought I might find the whole
thing interesting, but I barely heard a word. Over

waffles in a coffee shop Susan confessed she didn't hear a word, either. The lawyer did seem to get into a frenzy at one point, surmising how easy it would be for Susan to "clean house."

Susan's mother insisted on being present. She'd grown heavier since the last time I'd seen her. She carried many Hershey bars in her purse and had no shame about extricating them throughout the meeting.

Many years ago at Susan's and my college graduation ceremony, Susan's mother approached me and asked, "So what do you plan to do with your life?" It was rather a curse as I recollect it now. I suppose she felt her daughter was wasting her time with me. There were certain books I hadn't read that I was repeatedly asked about. When leaving the law office, her mother turned to me and said, "I'm sorry about your bad piece of luck."

Although we were in a small elevator and it was the ultimate wrong time to ask, I thought I'd try her. I said, "I've been thinking a lot about the principle of detachment. Do you know? Have you any position in particular you hold on detachment?"

She surprised me by taking my question seriously.

"It's something that comes whether you like it or not. One learns to pretend. After a series of sharp disappointments we can't help but retreat. You make little settlements with yourself. You attach yourself to less and less. There's no judgment in it—fair play, actually, really, when you think of it. There are so many things I don't give a goddamn about anymore, it would take a week to list them. It's a pity, because I liked Bill. I liked many things about him, but I can't have him making my little girl unhappy. When I hear Susan crying I feel my head split open. I will not tolerate it! Bill will pay, pay, pay. That is detachment. A series of choices, hot and cold choices, the amalgamation of which constitutes life. In a nutshell."

She got into a cab and sped away. Susan wasn't listening. She knew her mother's rap inside out. Now she wanted waffles or griddle cakes, anything with syrup.

After our late breakfast we thought we'd try our luck at the movies. But it was the usual car chases, car crashes, car explosions. We walked out. It was raining.

We went back to the apartment; Susan wanted to collect some jewelry and a few dresses she missed. She held up a big yellow chiffon thing she called her "daffodil dress." "I'm going to get a lot of use out of this!" she said sarcastically.

I was surprised to see the Doorman so unchanged. I'd always known he was Death, but now it was so obvious. Unmoving, unchanging, deliberate, malicious, sleepless, old, stinking of the profession. His uniform needed dry cleaning. He smiled at us as we entered the building—as if to say, "Smashed lives are my specialty—come closer."

There were a lot of packages that should have gone to the country house but somehow got sidetracked here—guest towels, guest linens, bathroom stuff. Although there were robust-looking towels in the house, Susan said she didn't want to be drying herself with some dead person's towel.

We went to Mag's office.

She had the hook rug on the wall. She said if she took it home it would be soaked with cat pee in no time. She asked Susan if she might want to do an update piece on crumbling marriage. It could be autobiographical or not; it could be a *meditation* on the subject, she said. Attack it any way you want. You don't have to use Bill's name. You can even write it like a poem. The only thing you can't do is use the word "fuck."

"Hector, did you notice my assistant Joseph isn't around?" asked Mag.

"Did he die?"

"No, darling, he didn't die. Don't be so morbid. Something better. He went to Switzerland."

"Really. His first trip? He won't like it."

"*Hector*, listen when good news is being given to you! Susan, I don't know how you put up with him. Tell him he's not going to get anywhere with that checked-out look on his face."

"You're not going to get anywhere with that checked-out look on your face," Susan reiterated, intonation-free.

"He's gone to Switzerland to have his blood flushed out. A wizard doctor there is giving some kind of mechanical blood bath, replacing all the infected cells with vegetables and minerals. I'm not sure of the details, but supposedly he's going to soon move the whole operation to London, so the time to go do it is now. I believe the first flushing is five thousand dollars, but then you get to take the solution home with you to self-administer. The only drawback is you have to inject it into your muscles, and that hurts a bit. Kent was so sweet, he volunteered at his own expense to accompany Joseph to Switzerland, but then Joseph's father said he'd go, isn't that sweet?"

Susan immediately wanted to call the airlines to see what kind of flights were available. She would not only accompany me to the clinic but be present during all injections and transfusions and insisted on funding the whole experiment.

Because we weren't complete fools, we got four of the names of persons who'd done the treatment and had enthusiastically recommended it to Joseph.

We called them, the men who'd taken the blood bath.

Two were dead; a third said he withdrew from the treatment because the muscle injections were unbearable. You had to find your own accommodations, and the hotels in the district were extremely expensive. His understanding of it was, it seemed to work at first but relapse followed rapidly. He said not to go and added in a very businesslike way, postpone no legal matters—did I have my will in order? Did I know the usual right-to-die form was not legal in New York State, that I would need another form with the name of a "health care proxy" on it as well as a substitute should the proxy become incapacitated, dead, or otherwise unavailable?

The fourth person could not be reached.

We decided to postpone any further plans until Joseph returned.

It was difficult deciding to go back to the country house, because it all looked so unfinished. When Bill walked out, all the work on the house came to a halt. The place looked very dramatic, with exposed ceilings, half-torn walls, and buckled floors.

We could have stayed with Susan's mother, it would have been convenient; but her apartment was small, with sharp objects and an impossible-not-to-notice pillow that said, "Fish and guests stink after three days."

We took the train. The tickets were wrong. The tickets are always wrong. We were told we had tickets for the slow train but we were on the fast train. We were sitting in the wrong direction, too, so that instead of feeling we were speeding into our future, it seemed the whole world—the gray river, the lush green trees, the stray ducks, half-gone docks, and soothing clouds—was losing itself, running backwards. There were other places to sit, but we didn't feel like getting up.

I could tell Susan was disappointed we couldn't go in good conscience to Switzerland. It would have been nice to have a project. Maybe not; maybe just to buy a cuckoo clock.

I liked that Mag said I looked "checked-out"; it counted as a sort of success. Was it the look of the detached I had now? Emaciated of ambition? I tried some little prayer in the taxi from the station to the house.

"Susan, don't you see I'm losing my mind? How I forget things, hardly speak, and when I do, repeat myself? What am I going to do, Susan? What am I going to do?"

Some ceiling fell down to underscore my point. It was funny. Susan did a hula around the smoking plaster and we laughed some more.

TV Guide was harassing me about getting their empty guide to emptiness. Threats from creditors filled the mailbox. I scrawled on the back of one, "I did not order *TV Guide* because I never would and I never will. I am ill and you are harassing me. Desist!" Jury-duty notices? I scrawled across the jittery forms, "AIDS!" Gyp-savings long-distance phone plans, the same; I shouted, "AIDS! AIDS! AIDS!"

In my bedroom was a little yellow note, gummed along one edge, in Kim's delicate if mad handwriting: "Emergency call Bill."

As it turned out, Bill was in the hospital having his left ball removed. Odd, it recalled my own wobbly testicle examination.

"My left nut is cancerous!" cried Bill on the telephone.

He wanted me to be there when he came out of the anesthesia. You're to hire a driver, he said, and gave me his car service number.

He was terrified.

"Oh, Bill," I said, "you have nothing to worry about. Doctors are experts at this sort of thing. They're always cutting someone's balls off. At certain hospitals it's a pet operation."

The first thing Bill said to me after the operation

was, "What a bad piece of luck this is!" The exact words of Susan's mother.

"Bill, the operation is a success."

"A success? I only have one ball left!"

"Bill, they just hang there, no one will notice. At the very worst you'll just have to switch to boxer-style swimming trunks instead of those minuscule little things you wear."

"What?"

"Calm down, Bill. You've just been through a stressful operation, and I assure you, agitating your mind will not help your scrotum."

"Hector, you just don't understand this! This is out of your league. And I don't mind telling you! When a woman makes love to a man, she expects certain equipment to be present and functioning. Am I making myself clear?"

There's always more than a droplet of hetero-sexual chauvinism in these sorts of exchanges.

"Bill, I know for a medical fact, your right ball can do the work for your gone left one as well as its own job. Potency and sperm production will re-main unaffected."

"You just don't get it!"

To change the subject I bring up Susan's and my visit to the divorce lawyer. He couldn't care less. He believes she will come crawling back.

Bill was grateful none of his tart-girlfriends got grapevine information on his sudden absence from the satyr circuit. Likewise his sexual-compulsive clubmates stayed away in packs. Male-female genital problems were the fearsome bogies of the paranoid and horny.

His dinner tray arrived, a gray shape stinking of disinfectant. It was all very familiar. House of Luck: bring your personal chow mein for quick takeout.

The nurses seemed to recognize me as someone marked by their disservices. An international melange of ethnicities, the Asians and Irish slightly more friendly. When an attractive young nurse in a brief uniform entered the room, Bill became absurdly flirtatious, lowering his voice and suggestively scratching his chest. I suppose this new level of male theater would now more or less permanently enter his repertoire. The nurse was surprisingly accommodating, shifting her costume around as if to simultaneously thwart and encourage denuding.

Out in the street it was raining again. Wishing to think less of the testicular, I ducked into a movie theater. I would swear on a stack of new Bibles the same movie Susan and I walked out of was playing, but with another title.

Thank God, I thought, one of the spiritual uplifters was speaking at Town Hall.

Because I was alone, even though I was late, I got a good seat.

She had gotten more attractive with the enormous success of her book. She wore a smart suit, lizard sandals, and an ankh around her neck, like the one on the cover of *The Love Machine* by Jacqueline Susann.

Her opening address took from the familiar terrain concerning the miserable unreality of this
world. She had a very convincing argument about
why relationships don't work. Of course I thought
of Bill and Susan. After the inspiring speech and
the pleasant hand-holding prayer section, question-
and-answer period began. Souls in widely varying
states of torment asked everything from "Why
doesn't my boyfriend ever call me?" to "How come
all my friends are dead and I'm not?"

Surprising myself, I stood up to speak.

I said, "I don't believe fear of death is primary
to the ill person. I think it's fear of suffering; suffering is the awful constant of life. To some extent I am
able to bear the various tortures of spinal tap, bone
marrow biopsy, bioscopy, colostomy, but the deepest
horror is the bitterness I feel welling up in me. It's
particularly poisonous now that I so desperately
need serenity. It's this bitterness that I feel is somehow built into everything. I see it in you too."

"Are you in a twelve-step program?"

"No."

"Are you an alcoholic?" she persisted, trying to
pin it all on the bitterness of the drunk.

"No."

"You have AIDS, don't you?"

"Yes."

"And something tells me you were like this
before you ever got AIDS. Is that true?"

"Yes."

"And my hunch is you got this it's-all-shit attitude from one of your parents. Your mother. What's your name?"

"Hector."

"Let's do a prayer chain. Does everyone know what a prayer chain is? Tonight we're going to pray for Hector and for Cathy's brother in prison and for Myra's operation and for—is it Arlene?—for Arlene's chemo and for Judd's mother at St. Luke's and for Mel at St. Vincent's and Rita who's left this dimension and Paul and Diane and Marie and Bruce and David and . . ."

I had very mixed feelings about her attack-oriented, skip-the-therapist type of spirituality. For example, the man weeping for his lost friends was told that he was just a slow learner. I rather hated the spiritual uplifter. She was probably right about everything, but the fact she was not ugly or marred in some way made it very difficult to absorb her drift.

It was still raining outside and too late to go back to the hospital.

I would spend the night in Bill and Susan's old apartment.

There were so few places to go. One moved from hideaway A to hideaway B, stopping at one or another hospital, exhausted by doctors pushing your pegs around the board.

It was worse than that. It seemed like there were only five or six people in the whole world. When you pick those people, I'll tell you, you'd better like them; you might be seeing an awful lot of them.

"You're in denial about my illness," I said to Susan.

"What?—No."

"If I say my feet hurt, you say your feet hurt too."

"They do!"

"If I say I'm going to die, you say we're all going to die."

"We are!"

"You're going to miss me horribly, Susan. You wait and see, it's going to be much worse than you imagine."

"Torturer! What do you need from me? Is my life not mangled-up enough for you? I'm not yet forty and I feel dog shit has been sprayed on every aspect of my life! Bill only had one testicle removed—pity! Had I been approached I could have saved his insurance company thousands of dollars in surgery costs! Denial? I dream about denial! I pray, 'Let denial come and fuck the living daylights out of my brain!' I'm going to kill myself, Hector. Yes—now or later. A woman unlucky in love can't hold a job. A woman unlucky in love is a dead duck. Who's going to contradict me?"

I decided to sleep in Susan and Bill's old bed. The sheets felt so cool. The cleaning woman must have just changed them.

The windows are of a double thickness, but I am hearing loud yelling from down below. *"To the right! . . . The right, not the left! . . . Sharp right! . . . Now left. . . . Left!"* Could it be the Doorman directing traffic into his little Hades at the bottom of the building? The old washing machines and dryers were there, but after several unsolved rapes and a slashing, the basement was shut to the tenants.

I was still dreaming when the telephone rang the next morning. It was Mag.

"You're there," she said. "Where's Susan?"

She had bad news: Joseph died. His father called from Europe. So maybe it wasn't such a good idea to go to Switzerland.

"Don't let this news be an opportunity for you to beat up on yourself. Because out of every piece of bad news comes good news too. Joseph worked for me for five years—no, six years come September—and I never even knew he had a daughter! A *daughter*. I immediately thought Kent and I should adopt her, but then I was told she was twenty—that's too old. It's a great loss for me, tell Susan. It's not just a marvelous assistant but a very close friend. This epidemic is really bringing out everyone's true colors. I don't see it as just a lot of rotten luck, I see it as a doorway into the New Age. Did I wake you?"

I was never young because no one wanted to be young with me.

GEORGES BERNANOS

———

Recollections

What day of the week is it?

I know I got in here on Tuesday.

Dehydration. Doctor said it was an emergency. But he seems to have so little clout I had to wait twelve hours in the emergency ward for a bed. When I was finally wheeled into a room, it was an empty room with six empty beds. A research team had decided it was best to keep people with the same diseases in the same room.

The last person I spoke with was a screeching woman in the cot next to mine in the emergency ward. We were divided by a gauze screen. "I'm being prejudiced against because I have AIDS and I look like a man! I'm so skinny and have a mustache only because I have AIDS!" And so forth, a top-volume harangue against everyone and everything, lumped and dubbed AIDS. I said to her, softly from beyond the screen, "If you relax and keep quiet you can find your center and the peace there." After a hoarse pause, she shouted, "What joke book did you get that out of?!"

That was the last person I spoke with. Some people came to visit me; I know it because there's a vase of peonies here. And a potted lily. A little late for Easter. I'm not talking.

I've entered a world I hate very much. The world of the past.

Oh, I didn't mind telling you about Noh and how Noh was a downbeat projection of some of my own funny aspirations.

"Noh," I'd said, "I wish you well from the bottom of my heart."

I thought God might vacillate between the two of us and slip me by. The message growing up was that if one took a wrong turn here and a wrong turn there suddenly one could be lost.

I'd long ago decided the past was an arbitrary handicraft of strung-together gewgaws, designed to strangle you or just hang limply around your neck. When I first saw a psychotherapist I took great delight in telling lies. I was a shoplifter. I'd been molested by relatives of both sexes. I was sold in North Africa as a male bride. I was made to wear a wedding gown and ride a camel. I drank blood.

But the past is very difficult to make up. Even if you are completely drunk or bombed out of your mind on one madness or another. It's a little crusade—in all cases, a children's crusade.

It's happening now. I can't stop it.

My face is down in the grass.

I'm in a broken-down hotel with my grandfather. With ingenuity I've sent my parents and sister to Niagara Falls to remarry their irritating banalities.

I'm obsessed with some teenagers here, boys and girls. Trying to learn the very latest dance steps, the very latest songs. They are sick of me. In a display of brutality, they take my chewing gum, my Chiclets, and toss them back and forth over my head. I leap and jump for the little yellow box, but the ridicule of it is too much, and I fall facedown in the grass.

My marauders disperse and my grandfather's brother picks me up by the shoulders and promises we will go fly a kite. He is a very ancient man, looking twice the age of my grandfather, who gets revitalized gambling at a card table up behind the hotel. It is a hotel of immigrants mostly, and their adult children: the food eagerly foreign, and the conversation nourished by memories of those left behind in the "old country." The few packs of teenagers with their mod details provide the little idiosyncratic allure available in the mountains.

I see Susan is here. In my hospital room, but not talking.

She's brought a huge pile of expensive magazines. Home, house, food, cuisine, clothes, fashion, style, commentary, gossip, profiles, slanders, horoscopes, benedictions, bric-a-brac, jewelry.

She hands me a magazine so we each have one to stare at, turning the pages with infinite patience, never commenting, occasionally ripping out a particular page, perhaps to maintain an earthly charade of giving a shit. This page has some dynamic piece of fabric, this page a wristwatch you can throw yourself into the ocean wearing.

After a hundred years we are joined by Bill's best friend, Bob, and his now-estranged-now-reconciled wife, Aileen.

The funny thing is, they don't acknowledge I'm in the room. Sure, they've got a little box in their hands of those miniature candied half-moons of red, yellow, orange, and green sugar, but they wave it around and never hand it to me.

"Susan, you can't let yourself get stuck in this. It's a sickness, wallowing in the waters of a rocky marriage. You and Bill have to get back together. Bob and I are making the effort—you and Bill can do the same," urged Aileen.

"I just bought a boat," Bob said, relating to the rocky waters.

"The marina is beautiful."

"There's room for four, and we can go the whole weekend, eat fish we catch right off the side of the boat."

The nurse comes in to take my temperature.

The thermometer has its own personalized plastic sleeve, which the nurse disposes of after saying, "It's broken."

"Susan, how many years have I known you? I know you inside-out, you keep forgetting that. You indulge these depressions and then you regret later all the time you've wasted. When I recollect all the time, money, and energy *I* wasted during that extended period of drug addiction, I just want to kick myself. I'm lucky to be alive," said Aileen.

Since Aileen and Bob would never look each other in the eye and Susan wouldn't look at them and no one would look at me, it appeared anyone who spoke spoke only to himself.

My IV pulls a little. The IV nurse will be here this evening to switch arms. They are using something called a Landmark catheter, which doesn't need to be switched as often from arm to arm and is considerably less invasive than the Hickman catheter, which is surgically implanted in your chest as a ready conduit to liquid nutrition, medicine, and blood.

In college there was an annual festival in a field celebrating the freshman who'd hung himself there ten years previously. Garbage pails filled with a mixture of wine and LSD gave the crowd a peek into the abyss the festival celebrated. Why am I remembering this? Oh, the green grass up against my face. Tripping. College. Susan. Aileen.

"Don't you remember right after college, Susan?" continued Aileen in more or less the same masculine-whiny voice her husband used. "We traveled. We went everywhere. All over Europe. I recollect the trip so vividly, Susan! Nothing impressed you. Nothing. Is that healthy? On the Amalfi coast two gorgeous playboys picked us up on their yachts and she acted like this happened every day. Boys passing in smaller boats sold us squid. And we cooked the squid right on board!"

A small argument begins and nearly never ends about how to cook squid so it doesn't get tough.

Bob says to bread the squid. Aileen dredges it through flour. One sprinkles it at the last moment with vinegar; the other makes a dip. The numbing debate comes to an end when Bob gives a sickening recipe for squid stuffed with hard-boiled eggs.

"Talk to us, Susan! We've come all this way to this lousy hospital to see you—acknowledge us!"

"She wouldn't even visit Bill in the hospital with his testicular problem. She's a selfish bitch," Bob spewed.

"Speak, Susan! You are an evil witch. Suffer in silence." Aileen, for the first time all afternoon, turns to me. She has salt-and-peppered her short hair, is wearing athletic gear and a lot of inappropriate jewelry. Bob's dressed similarly but grips his crotch habitually, certainly to make sure both balls remain intact.

"You don't look bad, Hector," Aileen continues. "I mean it. You've attained a certain angelic beauty with all your weight loss. Your skin is beautiful. I never liked you built up from all that compulsive exercise. Bodybuilders walk like windup dolls. It's vulgar, too—an externalized plea for sex. I tell Bob he has to stay out of the sun more. You see how his skin is going?"

"Do you know what I heard?" says Bill. "I heard Drano kills the AIDS virus in the lab. You know— the drain unclogger."

"Worth a try. Bob's cousin Justin is involved in urine therapy. I don't know the whole story, but he urinates all over himself."

"Don't be absurd, Aileen—he *drinks* the urine. He says it's very pure, and he's the only one of his circle of friends who isn't dead. Fresh urine is un- explored territory."

"Pee might be a panacea."

After Aileen and Bob leave, Susan and I ex- change silent congratulations, having achieved the rude but exhilarating rush of ignoring two jerks.

Like a relay in a sports event, we pass magazines back and forth and fall back into supreme quiet, in- terrupted only by a nurse stating the flowers stink.

In the seventh grade there was a girl named Bonnie who was obsessed with Edgar Winter of the band Edgar Winter's White Trash. She stripped the color of her hair to pillowcase white and kept her skin aspirin-colored in all seasons. All this to look like Edgar Winter.

Unlike Edgar Winter and most of the girls in her seventh-grade class, Bonnie was quite bosomy, and extremely sexy in her skintight white lace blouses. To every party Bonnie would bring an undercooked white cake. Many said she was having sexual rela- tionships with members of the band.

Bonnie's behavior was attributed to her mother's death midyear, but I don't remember her ever being different. Having endured a fairly restrictive upbringing myself, I admired Bonnie's freedom to attend late-night concerts and appear as her own fantasy. Her grades weren't very good, but I thought, So what? I see now Bonnie was the prototype for Susan Ded.

Two people who are to become great friends recognize on first contact their mutual flaws. The conglomeration of those flaws amounts to a wedding of sympathies and reassuring prejudices. It was a not particularly unusual case of a straight woman preferring the company of a gay man and a gay man preferring the company of a straight woman. Susan would even take me out on dates—I mean *with* her dates, the three of us. It would take a pretty sturdy fellow not to feel mocked and challenged under our scrutinizing, opaque joviality.

It wasn't as if we sat around discussing clothes all day or anything like that. No, we made fun of Hemingway blabbering on some tape we had to listen to for our Lost Generation class, and of Yeats as an old man getting monkey-gonad implants for potency, and of various life-hating poets whose suicides crystallized their knack for isolation. We rather adored a particular lady poet whose bad but brilliant poet husband burned the bulk of her journals, thus, somehow, perfecting her mythology of supreme victim. As the coup de grâce to the real-life story, his death-camp-survivor girlfriend copycatted the wife and stuck her own head in an oven. He's married to a nurse now, the husband. A poet laureate, I believe.

Wasn't the nurse just here? She gives me a needle, examines the flow of the IV, and makes some torturing small talk about poor pay. When we don't respond, she insists visiting hours are over (as well they must be) and Ms. Ded must leave.

I ask for the zillionth time for a second blanket.

"Peace of God, Peace of God," utters a bloodshot priest like a Lower East Side vendor. Our unorthodox eyes frighten him away. Susan kisses me goodnight and shuffles out.

Have I mentioned she has begun to drink?

I've always been fascinated by the process by which a person begins to drink. No expert on the subject, I've soberly observed people who have no problem with it having quite a large problem with it. Sudden, gradual, mysterious, obvious, sad, scary, boring. When Susan put all Bill's things in a big black plastic garbage bag next to his car, she went back into the house and poured herself an extremely tall glass of clear liquid from a liquor bottle. Yes, clicking of ice went through the day, and then through most days following.

When we were still talking a bit, a cool detachment entered our afternoon paralysis. Is that all it takes? All this turgid pursuit of detachment and all it took was an early cocktail, olive and everything.

"It's so quiet suddenly. So peaceful," Susan said on the porch of the house at dusk. "Don't you feel so quiet suddenly? And peaceful."

"Yes," I said, lying. My medication made me feel morning, noon, and night like a boat on its side in a squall.

"You don't think I'm an alcoholic, do you? Or, I mean, just becoming one?"

"No, no, of course not. Not at all. Alcoholics have a complete personality change when they drink, and you're just the same."

"That's right, I'm just the same. Only less thirsty. And I'm expecting less. Do you know? More peaceful. Expecting less than nothing. Very peaceful."

Peace of God . . . Peace of God.

Who said that now?

I'm dreaming. Lights out.

I'm with my grandfather again. He's winning at poker at the card table behind the hotel. Dense pines in the background. There's one woman gambler much younger than my grandfather's crowd. She's a compulsive in loud but trendy Capri pants. She's losing. Her children come to implore her; she chases them away harshly, not because she hates them but because she's ashamed. My grandfather gives me some of his winnings and I resolve to march to town solo and order an elaborate sundae.

At the counter of the old-fashioned soda shop I slowly spoon the walnut-encrusted ice cream into my thin mouth.

Woman behind the counter screws up her face to say, "Oh, *antisocial!*" The newspaper rack has papers with headlines like MARTIANS IMPREGNATE WOLVES. A comic book says, MILLIE THE MODEL TAKES OVER. I buy both. On the walk back to the hotel I cross a little bridge and stare down at the pebbly rush of water.

They've brought in another half-alive person. Younger. He's in for brain testing. He's in a considerably altered state. He asks me, "Is the AIDS crisis over?" "No," I say curtly. He is some kind of bigwig in ACT UP, someone who yells in front of the deaf White House.

His cute boyfriend comes in periodically and sits sullenly in the corner wearing a Walkman.

Outside the sealed window, below, there is a green garden. Marigolds, zinnias, a few roses. There'd been a larger, more extravagant garden a little distance away, entirely attended by volunteers. The hospital decided that the lush garden would be better used as a parking lot. The compensatory new garden, with its brick octagonal walls, looks like a parking lot also.

It's day again. Must be. The kick and shuffle of the day nurses resumes. My roommate is wheeled out for more brain testing.

He's missing all the cooking shows on TV. I like this one Indian woman who takes you on little walking tours of Hong Kong, tasting treats from steamy stalls. She kayaks down the filthy canals of Bangkok for lovely little satays and sweet, leaf-wrapped rice concoctions.

The other cooks are more disturbing. There's a very heavyset, senile man who occasionally has trouble breathing and always has trouble remembering things. He will start the show calling the meat a pork roast; then he says it's a veal roll; then he catches himself and calls it a pork roast again, and then a veal roll. He holds up an onion but he can't remember what it's called. He stares tragically at the root vegetable and says, "We'll use some of what this is."

I've fallen asleep again, thank God.

I've missed an IV change, thank God.

I'm dreaming.

Wet, dark, slick road. *Tip tap,* my shoes go. A desiccated old queen approaches me, tatters and grandeur. She says, quite distinctly, *"Hi, little boy. Are you lost?"* Hobbling a little closer, she says, *"You're on Joyless Street."*

I'm crying.

Why am I crying?

Who's asking me that question?

I'm crying for everything I've lost. Peanuts, pretzels, popcorn, pizza of God.

TV: "AIDS hopelessness prevails—more at eleven."

Susan has arranged for a masseur to come to the hospital room and work on me on the bed.

The masseur expertly removes my hospital smock, passing the IV sack through the sleeve. I'm the nude scarecrow I've come to know. For some insane reason he removes all his clothes too, declaring he does all his massages in the nude.

Shiatsu, Swedish, Tantric massage, he says by way of introduction. I protest that Shiatsu is painful, but he begins his pinching and pummeling, undressed and undeterred.

Susan is guarding the door from the outside.

Occasionally a nurse will tell her she can't sit there blocking the door and that the door must be open at all times. "Get fucked," Susan says, slightly inebriated from her recent lunch around the corner.

The massage does relieve some of my body aches, but I'm quite impotent now, with my libido buried under the weight of illness and medications. For this reason the Tantric part of the massage is omitted and my masseur, with an entirely shaven head and body, asks, "Do you ever have sex?" "No," I say, telling the truth. "Well," he says, "you should masturbate yourself slowly daily but not have an orgasm because the orgasm will release too much energy." Also, I should not wear white; I should wear red and take in more minerals in the autumn.

When my feelings are hurt even a little, I always have the sensation of falling down stairs.

Earlier in my disintegration, Bill, Susan, and I spent a weekend in East Hampton at one of Bill's clients' estates. The handsome property had multiple decks of gray slatted wood. A deck to the pool, a deck that said let's-sit-and-drink, another deck for midnight dining, and the deck the host was the most proud of, the one for *thinking*.

I was descending the thinking deck when my legs buckled and I fell down to the drinking deck.

My legs were toothpicks from my recent PCP hospital stay, where thirty pounds seemed to disappear overnight. It was a bad fall, and the people taking hors d'oeuvres on the drinking deck looked at me sympathetically but helplessly, knowing I would be lifted and removed to the convalescent deck, which wasn't actually a deck but a patio and on the only unappealing side of the house, in ghastly shade with unpromising plant life.

When I was eleven it seemed my parents were constantly dragging me to funerals. The dead people were referred to as relatives, yet at holiday gatherings there seemed no signs of attrition. A massive cast of peripheral characters existed nameless until dead.

Forty days after the person's death there would be a flounder-eating party, usually in the church basement. On this particular Sunday the memorial lunch was held in a cavernous old building with sweeping marble stairwells leading with rococo aplomb to individual apartments. The elevator wasn't well, so there were a lot of old people dressed in black on the stairwell.

Suddenly one of the mourners fell backwards, hands in the air like the detective in *Psycho,* and smashed on the marble landing. Unlike the detective in *Psycho,* the elderly woman was wearing a wig that flew off during her dramatic fall. Someone ran to stick the wig back on her bleeding head, as if this were a life-saving device. Half the crowd was thinking, Oh no, not another funeral! The other half was certainly cheering, Oh goody, more dark events, more flounder!

Indeed, no sooner were we home from this fish fry than my parents ran to their church calendar to scar up the date boxes with more wakes, more funerals, more fish. I lost my temper. I shouted, "We don't even know her!" "Not know Mrs. *Stef-*

ouris?!" my mother stormed. It turned out Mrs. Stefouris had a now-also-dead cousin who had stuck some fur on the collar of my mother's "engagement" coat. The coat has survived decades of total neglect, but the collar is pretty ratty. Still, the coat is safe; my parents will not throw anything away, not found things or bought things or haphazardly attained things. My only explanation is they think they're going to live forever.

My sister's house has no extraneous object (and no place to sit). The whole time growing up I would ask her questions like "Do breasts give milk or something? Because all the paintings depict the Christ baby sucking at the Madonna breast." For this intelligent question I was consistently warned, "Don't believe everything you hear!"

Truly now I don't. Rote education is effective. I believe almost nothing I hear now.

Why am I thinking about them? It only makes me nervous.

Oh, right, falling down stairs.

I had a lousy little dream last night. Meant nothing.

Noh was all dressed up, with a little burnt doll of Maxwell Drake. You couldn't tell really that it was Maxwell Drake, because it was so charred and shrunken, but it was. Noh began to play with the tiny corpse like a puppet and gave it a singing voice. Old show tunes.

My newest shrink is here this morning. Uninvited. Dreams don't impress him much unless within them you are nuzzling the sex organs of one of your immediate relatives.

"I didn't want you to miss your appointment," he said. "Are you happy I'm here?"

"Happy?"

"Are you bored with me?"

"Bored with you?"

Even if it was only echolalia, I was talking some again.

"Do you want to talk about being in the hospital again?"

"No."

"Do you want to talk about Bill and Susan?"

Bill and Susan. Susan and Bill.

Billsan and Susill. Blah blah blah. She loves him and he loves her. She wants him and him wants whim. I want you and you do too. You and me and me and you. You and he and you and she and you and we. . . . Amen, rest in peace.

"Don't you feel our therapy is working?"

"Psychotherapy for the terminally ill is a little like a pedicure right before having both feet amputated."

"A lot of my patients have gone through terrible ordeals and, yes, even amputations. One fellow had terrible KS in his legs and they turned completely black and swelled to elephant size and, yes, we were forced to amputate, but now, I tell you, he's like Gandhi."

"Gandhi? Gandhi was a very active man who initiated great change in the history of his country. He wasn't sitting around taking pills and injections and admiring his amputations. I just don't see the connection."

"This sick boy became like a saint before he died. You should have heard his voice—it was so pure, purified. He was in a sixth-floor walk-up and in a wheelchair, but his spirit had lifted him up out of this realm."

"I see," I said.

Maybe he's going through that countertransference thing with me. It's where the therapist becomes dependent on the patient instead of vice versa.

I once was in a very bad situation with a shrink who really went off her rocker. She'd try to set up mystery dates for me in Damrosch Park and then say, oh, it was the wrong night but oh, she saw me there while she was hiding behind her program—I was wearing a blue shirt and brown jeans (who has brown jeans?!). Then she started sending me love notes—lots of them: "You are a treasure, you are a beauty!"

One of the things I liked about the hospital was the plastic jug you got to pee in without ever having to get up.

The trouble with those jugs was you had to get the nurse to empty them. "Nurse!" I'd call. "Nurse, I need to be emptied."

"Don't call me 'Nurse'! My name is Miss Miller! *Miss Miller.*"

The nurse stomped out of the room then, young and angry; jilted? I wondered.

"You may be getting out tomorrow," declared a little squadron of apprentice doctors. The oldest looked fourteen. They have that funny slant of the head that's supposed to mean "You po' thing!"

Good.

I can go out on the blind date with Susan.

With Juan.

Kent the zombie, of all people, set up the date, somehow reaching Susan and emphasizing what a rare and sensitive being Juan was (is).

Juan.

Sounds exotic. I hope he has lots of dinero. I'll suggest the overpriced Four Seasons.

It'll be nice if we can sit near the bubbling pool. I know for a fact the ice-cold heart of New York is drowned there. (Or maybe just mine.)

———

Radiation

Juan was nice.

I did convince Susan to wear a moss-colored sheath intricately sewn with opalescent beads. When she walked, she looked like a dark puddle radiating light. A flapper making her first appearance since her father's suicide. She looked good.

We couldn't get reservations at that other restaurant I mentioned. They were very particular about times and advance notice, especially if you wanted to be seated facing that pool no one can swim in anyway. We went to a place I never heard of, which was fine with me since I could drive the waiters and cooks crazy just as well anywhere.

I was so happy! Happy, yes, to be out of the hospital and free—I will never return there, no, I'll die facedown in the dirt rather than—

Both of the Deds, individually, had insisted on accompanying me out of the hospital on departure day. Susan just pretended Bill was invisible while Bill spoke eagerly on every subject, more like a punished son than a repentant husband. Finally he just shouted, "You don't even have the decency to ask about my balls!"

After we got all my junk into the car, we drove to the apartment, dropping Bill off at Bob's, where he agreed to hole up while Susan had her Manhattan business to accomplish. Also, it was established I needed a little while to regain my legs before returning to the war-torn country house.

Bill figured Susan had done nothing further to progress the divorce. He knew her mother and how it would require her to generate the speed of the legal dissolution of the marriage. He would bide his time; her mother was famously busy herself and, after the initial indignation and anger, perhaps was seeing the separation through more muted evaluation. Her mother, the detachment expert.

I don't think Susan would've agreed to the zombie Kent's blind-date maneuver if I hadn't seemed so enthusiastic about it. (There's no reason to continue referring to Kent as a zombie while Susan's somnambulism far outdoes any deadness Kent might radiate.)

Juan picked us up in his own car and miraculously parked it a step away from the restaurant.

He was of a handsomeness unique to certain gentlemen and ladies. Ageless. Lots of black hair on his head with daring little shocks of white at the temples. Lineless face. Hispanic, but impossible to locate from where; perfect diction. Puerto Rico? I didn't want to ask. Midnight blue blazer, dapper shoes.

At first I just started jabbering to cover for Susan, who ordered her cocktail as we entered the antechamber to the restaurant and before our reservations were verified. She gazed above that cocktail into outer space, the very empress of detachment. Weirdly, every now and then she would smile, as if she were understanding everything, or else receiving direction from unseen photographers.

I wasted no time. The appetizers hadn't even arrived when I said to Juan, "Juan, forgive me for chattering so mercilessly. You must think I'm some sort of mad monkey! But you have to understand I've been incarcerated recently and my freedom has made me quite drunk—hasn't it, Susan?"

Juan said, "You haven't been incarcerated, you've been hospitalized. Kent told me. I'm so sorry, and so pleased you felt the energy to join us tonight."

"Oh, thank you, Juan!" I said eagerly. I was turning from mad monkey to baby vampire bat. Oh Lord, would I spend the entire evening transmogrifying?

I continued, "You didn't think it peculiar that I was invited along? It is rather unorthodox, you must admit."

"No. I found it charming. Things were arranged so that I was meeting not one but two interesting people. I'm quite lucky."

The antipasto arrived, a phantasmagoria of little fried things. I pushed it to the side and plunged immediately into my now standard interrogation.

"Juan, I've been doing a lot of reading lately—well, not a lot, but intensely. Well, as intensely as I can—you see I wear an eye patch. I'm reading about detachment, detachment as a subject, actually as a spiritual discipline. I'm reading these essay-sermons by this mystical Meister Eckhart. I think that's how you say his name. Ever heard of him?"

"It's a concept that runs through most religions, through a great deal of religious thought. Detachment."

"Also known as indifference," I chimed in.

Susan flicked her hair and smiled as if this gesture contributed heavily to the discussion.

"Clearly we cannot attach ourselves to the things of this world. They are the only things we do not possess."

I was thrilled. Juan was intelligent and had an inner life; I would insist Susan go to bed with him!

"Juan," I said, "tell me your theory of prayer. I feel I'm such a novice at it that I botch up all my sporadic attempts."

"It's a discipline. Like any discipline—exercising or weeding the garden—it is at first unpleasant.

Paradoxically, one's soul itself resists the very exercise or chore that will render it to ecstasy. The weeded garden in full flourish may very well resemble heaven, or at least our earthly imagining of it."

"Are the weeds *sin?*" I asked. I'd only that morning finished reading a whole chapter on sin, and the world of it seemed decidedly defunct but marvelously organized hierarchically! The only time I'd ever heard the word "sin" used in conversation was when someone said it was a sin to waste good food.

Apropos of that, Susan was slyly removing all the squid from the antipasto platter and folding them into her linen napkin. Juan politely pretended not to notice but did make a dive toward a roasted red pepper when I used the word "sin."

"Did you know that a caper is a pickled flower bud?" I said to change the subject for a second.

"Yes, I knew," Juan answered semimystically.

Instead of sin we reviewed our menus. Susan pointed to her choice on the placard. Veal shank. Anomie hadn't affected her appetite. Although when the food did arrive, like most drunks she just pushed it around until dessert. Why won't she talk?!

"Susan's a brilliant speaker. You wouldn't know it but it's true. In college we had a professor—a real lulu—who made us stand up and read our papers aloud to the class. Susan read her prize essay on Romeo and Juliet. Everyone was enthralled."

"A very romantic choice," he said. Rather pedestrian remark, but elevated by the ecclesiastic velvet of his voice and the deep way he looked into her dead eyes when he said it.

I don't know what I ordered. I hated and loved everything now. Fish, fowl, red meat, live salads. I could eat everything and nothing; I took a breadstick.

Juan took Susan's hand, a little dead thing that didn't move. Oh, he's brilliant! I thought. They will be making love by midnight!

Suddenly I decided, I will watch! Yes! The obscene suggestion I'd so readily rejected from Bill I would now enact. We will finish dinner, linger over decaffeinated demitasse, and fly then to the adultery-seasoned bedroom of Bill and Susan. Susan will make some excuse to keep Juan in the kitchen for a few minutes, perhaps helping with the ice-cube trays, while I go to the bedroom to hide behind the tall decoupage screen, a screen of Victorian children and their furry pets.

Suddenly Juan looked up from his red steak and questioned me. I marveled how he could eat and hold her hand at the same time. Susan's free hand was glued to her vodka glass, afraid that waiters wanted whatever she had.

"Do you confuse detachment with resignation? I think perhaps you do. They are very different— opposite, in fact. Resignation defiles God. Detachment flatters him."

How horribly clear it was to me to hear this

truth! How I had spent my life always at the edge of the party! And now death would receive his favorite entree—the life unlived, a sour treat inflamed.

The sauce on Susan's veal was coagulating. I guess I'd ordered this milky dish of noodles and peas in front of me. I stared at it to keep from crying. I stirred the mixture. It was God's mind I was looking at! The peas and noodles.

"Juan, go on, say more!"

Susan's teeth glittered. She will devour him. Deadness must gravitate to goodness for its minimum sustenance. Juan prays; he's admitted as much. I listened to Juan.

"During the ordeal of Christ's Crucifixion, he was given a sponge of vinegar to sting his wounds. In fact, the sponge was soaked with a soporific poison. Christ shouted—'Lord, Lord, why hast thou forsaken me?' Then he lost consciousness. The Dead Sea Scrolls have revealed so much."

"Juan, if he was so high up on the cross, how did they get the sponge to him?"

"On a spear. It turns out the two thieves at either side of him weren't thieves at all—they were zealots, peoples of a politically threatening nature. The Romans never bothered to crucify thieves. Christ was tried as a zealot too and was revived in the tomb by the two other zealots, using an aloe mixture smuggled to them by Peter."

"The saint," I said, offering my slim expertise.

Waiters were beginning to loiter near our table: devotees, converts, gawkers—it was hard to distinguish which.

Our desserts arrived. Parfaits, the color of clouds in certain cinquecento paintings where Zeus is about to penetrate a nymph.

"Anyway, the point should be to emphasize the Resurrection, not the Crucifixion. The variety of human crucifixion is too wide for God to keep track of; resurrection is always the same—"

"Transcendental elevation of the spirit," I said, echoing something I'd picked up somewhere.

"That is correct," said Juan, his flock dispersing. Were these blasphemous notions? I couldn't know.

I excused myself, hobbling between the tight lane of eaters stopping to stare.

In the men's room a lanky, elderly man in a silver suit was standing there doing nothing. He was too elegant to be a molester.

"I have no time," he said to me. "Terrible to waste an old man's time. Terrible and expensive. Good luck."

I had no time, either, especially for interpreting omens. I took from my pocket the card I had taken from the table of matches and toothpicks and on the reverse wrote a short message, instructions for Susan.

Running back to the table, having forgotten to pee, I handed the card to her. "Susan, I *know* you'll want to *save* this so you can return again and again to this lovely eatery."

She freed her Juan hand, vodka hand holding fast, flipped over the card, glancing at the message, slipped it into her tiny purse, and laughed in Juan's face (he was tabulating the bill) and then started harassing the waiter for not bringing fresh plastic straws. Despite what I said about her Bergmanian silence, she will do that—speak suddenly and forcefully if she really wants something.

As we pulled up to the apartment and parked, Juan didn't need further communication; Susan was smiling and licking her lips in a near-psychotic fashion.

She tripped over her heel at the entranceway, laughed, and stepped out of her shoes. Juan was quick to bow down and collect them. He was smiling now too, obviously aroused. Doorman leering.

The elevator swung slightly from its cable, cranking, participatory.

In the sea-green corridor to the apartment, Susan pinned Juan to the wall. She was kissing him full-mouthed, swinging her head back and forth.

She laughed again and said, very loudly, "Hector's going in first, before us. To *ventilate* the place before we go in. Okay? Hector, you go in, and after you've *successfully* ventilated, go to bed. Say goodnight to Juan."

"Goodnight, Juan."

I ran into the apartment, put on my pajamas, chucked down a fistful of my usual pills, and then stationed myself securely behind the decoupage screen, shining strangely in the blackened bedroom.

By the time Juan and Susan entered the room, they were both practically undressed, garments hanging off their shoulders, caught around their necks and ankles.

I must say Susan was making a lot of noise. For a recent deadhead, she was about as lively as a human gets.

In no time they were on the bed, nude, entwined, in full swing.

It was good to see Juan's ardor was in no way affected by his strong spiritual convictions. I was glad.

I even sneezed twice behind the screen, but their noise drowned me out. Crouched there in my pajamas, I thought maybe this was a good time to try some more praying. (Juan said his aunt would come over at a moment's notice to pray with me, and I didn't doubt she'd have a talent for it.)

Dear Lord, save us! We don't know you and you don't know us, but hear our inner voices calling from the burning building of misfortune! Say we are not to be singed beyond repair!

By the time I'd finished my prayer the lovemaking was dying down. I was glad that body-slapping sound had come to an end, as I found it unpleasantly evocative of the past. Juan was more exhausted than Susan, but they'd both shared an enormous number of orgasms, at one point sounding like two people being strangled.

Susan sat up, staring at the black screen. The room was roasting now from air-conditioner neglect and stank too of their combined juices. I was getting sleepy and would sleep probably behind the screen if Juan didn't rise for a toilet visit.

Hair is matted this way and that across Susan's face. She is more alive than usual at this moment, the sweat on her face working to create a luminosity. Is Juan snoring?

I think I know what Susan is thinking. No, I *know* what Susan is thinking:

What has happened to me? I was a beautiful woman and now my face is a contortion of unhappiness. I want back what I have lost! I want back what was stolen from me! It can't be enough to say I've made some grave error of judgment. Death in life is too severe a punishment for any error. Or did I gravitate to Bill with the impulse to kill what was an innate love of beauty—the beauty of the spirit?! Bill isn't exactly an ogre, but he is a man who naturally gravitates to filthiness. I am a simpleton! To beg for one's punishment and then to scorn its total arrival! Like Saint Helen (it is Saint Helen, isn't it?), I should like my tongue cut out so I should never speak and betray my horrendous simpleness. No one must know. . . .

I drifted off to sleep then, crumpled behind the screen, not uncomfortable.

When I awoke Juan had already gone. Susan was in the shower, whistling, of all things.

Creakingly I made my way to the kitchen to grind up my two DDI tablets in the blender. It comes out powdery and I mix it with four ounces of water. The taste is chalky like an antacid, only with a shrapnellike aftertaste.

After that I crawled to my usual guest bed.

When I awoke it was September. I leaned over to the window to see what September was doing. August had been a long rainstorm and then changed its mind the last minute and regained its old personality of humid stasis.

The sun is out now. No clouds.

I've had a relapse of my CMV. IV pump again. Home-care nurses in and out of the apartment, more blood work, vein adjustments.

The first round of nurses were oddly tarted-up Dominican women complaining of their teenaged daughters' wild ways. They were dazzled by the Ded apartment and explored (with my encouragement) every nook of it.

My next nurse was Perry from Liverpool. Perry was a kindly man who sat with me two hours while we unkinked the coil in the catheter in my arm. He spoke very bitterly of his years in London nursing drug addicts. He said methadone was no more than a big scam to make the hospitals rich. Addicts, he said, absolutely couldn't stand to have any procedure that involved a needle unless it was specifically a "pleasure needle."

I asked him about disintegration, how far one had to go to finally let go.

Suicide was not a taboo subject with Perry. He quickly released the recipe to something called the Brompton Cocktail, named after the hospital it was widely used in, for "pain anxiety in terminal-care patients." Recipe: heroin syrup, a little phenobarbital, a little cocaine, all mixed in an alcohol base. Shake well.

He spoke with yet more enthusiasm about the IV Potassium Push. The patient is first given an injection of fentanyl, an anesthetic agent, followed then by the lethal (and severely stinging without the first numbing shot) injection of potassium. The Potassium Push.

These drugs and procedures are not so easy or accessible on their own. A sympathetic doctor could prescribe the morphine derivative Dilaudid (4 mg size), and if the patient should take one hundred and twenty capsules, preceded by about five suppositories of an antivomiting agent called Compazine, then all one needed, losing consciousness, was to have "a friend" tie a plastic bag over your head.

My regular doctor could not stand this subject and would not converse upon it. He didn't say so, but I'm sure he considered it an insult to his profession. On the other hand, he began to love the subject of radiation. Radiation was suggested to me at each visit.

Radiation to melt away your KS lesions, my doctor urged, had no guarantees. They could reappear as capriciously as they'd first appeared. In the spirit of investigation, I telephoned someone I knew who was getting a lot of radiation, and it turned out he was having his foot (which had not responded to the radiation and was swollen and black) amputated that morning. (A Gandhi hopeful?)

Juan's aunt never came to pray with me. She was a full-time cook for *Newsweek* and cooked for her private shaman on weekends.

Juan was nice.

But I hardly saw him. He and Susan dated and they always asked me to join them, but I just felt too tired. Maybe I became disappointed (resigned) about him. I don't know what I expected, but I think now he was only a successful blind date and, for Susan, a superb lay.

One night when they were going out I stopped them in the hall and I challengingly asked Juan, "Does amputation count as crucifixion? Because I know someone who was all amputated this morning. A successful ladies-swimsuit designer."

Neither one answered me; I got a small hug as a compensatory kiss-off.

The sour taste in my mouth made me think of the Man with the Silver Attaché Case.

I know something about sexual dependency.

I had to keep my armpits unclean even though I have always been a cleanliness type of person. He was deeply committed to deeply kissing my behind. This is a sexual habit I for one have never even tried, although its performance on me was to be repeated in Milan by a guard at *The Last Supper*—being restored at that time but open still for delectation.

The Silver Attaché was filled with money. The young man worked furiously accruing cash by computer punching through the night. They pay you more than double if you work this graveyard shift. The money was to live in some city—Barcelona, I think. The deal was I didn't even have to say "I love you" or even "I'll stay with you." I merely had to say "I'll go" or else that he should stay. (I consulted Noh at the time, who said just say no.)

He cried at my feet, calling me heartless. (It must prove his point that I cannot today recall his name.)

When I would penetrate his soft white ass he would always choose that moment to moan, "Oh Hector, I love you." Love could not be so directly connected to the prostate. Could it?

"You will fall in love this fall with one of your students. I know it!"

"Now, how or why could I do that when I have someone so sensitive, intelligent, and beautiful to take to bed? I'd be a fool."

"Oh, darling!" he'd say.

My psychiatrist says not to do radiation, that radiation performed on a suppressed individual will more likely than not cause more damage than good.

I must say Susan's semirevival hurts my brain— an unmeetable challenge to my irreversible decline.

If only it all were psychiatric. I should begin shock therapy this afternoon. I should perform my frontal lobotomy with my own two hands and be glad of it. I should thank my nurses as they lace up my straitjacket and thank them, my doctors, after six months of learning how to use a fork properly and passing through a series of ascending wards named after deciduous trees. I should very well thank God then and feel blessed.

(I'd better hang up now.)

> This race is precisely the flight from creatures to union with the uncreated.
>
> DIONYSIUS THE AREOPAGITE

———

Bill

At the first of the several colleges Bill was expelled from, he committed a violent crime.

The college had an English-style pub called the Pub. A bar on campus, the administration must have thought, would discourage students from seeking alcohol in town. Bill was like many of the beer-guzzling Pub-goers: inebriation uncovered a streak of violence. Some nudge was annoying him, so Bill picked up a wood bench and clobbered the poor undergraduate, cracking the boy's skull and giving him a concussion.

All sorts of legal actions were put on hold pending the medical progress of the bashed boy. The school was adamant about making a point about drinking and violence; they insisted Bill leave.

Though the boy recovered and his parents' cravings for retribution were lulled by gratitude, Bill suffered terribly, guiltily trudging from school to school. Finally, because the college prided itself on its liberal ways, Bill was allowed, wholly repentant, to return to the institution of his former rage.

The odd thing was, he was really cured. He never again got smashed drunk or struck another human being. The only misdemeanor he was party to before graduation was participating in a fraternity gangbang of the new English professor's wife. Although the administration, the professor, and everyone else heard of this wild night of orgiastic fulfillment, no official action was taken, because the wife, a redhead with tiny breasts, had willingly entered the fraternity house at midnight and admitted to inciting the whole scene, orchestrating a lot of partner shifting. The only one who suffered in the end from this excess was the professor, who, predictably, could only mumble his lectures on Jane Austen, Nathaniel Hawthorne, and William Congreve for six months until his thoughts on manners, guilt, and cuckoldry could regain composure.

When Bill described the "party" to me, he seemed particularly proud of the homosexual feature of the postadolescent boys standing around naked with shiny erections. I thought he was only saying that for my benefit, but when he repeated it ten times I had to conclude this element of it had indeed given him pleasure.

I've been at Bill's since last Friday. This whole Juan thing started to get on my nerves. His relationship with Susan got more and more intense in its own weird way, and Juan refused to have any more theological talks with me. I resented the fact Susan seemed to liven up for a stranger named Juan when she would hardly talk to me. But that's always the way, isn't it? A little physical tenderness and the big meltdown begins.

Even though I'm shriveling up before my eyes, I begrudge no one his pleasures. More about that in a minute, when I go on about Bill's latest whores. (They were instructed to kick him around the living room shouting "Filthy shithead!") But first let me tell you what I found among Susan's scarves and tangled jewelry. Her book! The book she said she might write about me!

There wasn't much of it, but what there was blew my mind. I know we don't all see ourselves exactly the way others see us, but it was a revelation that my best friend should depict me as I don't know what—Madame Defarge crossed with Soupy Sales!

And the writing style! It reminded me exactly of *The Shining* where the jumpy wife finally sees just what Jack Nicholson has been up to at the typewriter and it's one sentence repeated a thousand times. Well, it was at this moment I decided I could be just as nontraditional as Susan and write my own book, keep the same subject, me, and really do no worse. Use the diary form, more or less. Try to steer clear of the memoir form—oh!

I yelled at Susan. I told her it was a gratuitously unpretty picture she'd drawn (half-drawn) of me, and I didn't appreciate it!

She didn't cry or anything, but I imagine her confidence as a writer didn't allow her much of a defense.

"Burn it," she suggested.

"Damn right I'll burn it—and the whole house with it!—Depicting me as some medieval puppet—!"

I was glad to get away from the country house. Although the trees hadn't begun their full masquerade, the leaves were already tinged with death. At least in Manhattan changes of seasons licked their wounds in private. (Sometimes you didn't even know if it was snow or just a lot of ashes flying around.) I spent most of my time in the apartment. Some of Bill's cronies from his horny gentlemen's club came to the apartment in support of Bill. They encouraged him to pick up old bad habits.

My strongest feeling sitting there on the gray couch was vividly nihilistic; I thought, Why isn't everyone just dead? Not just me—everyone.

Bill's arrogance dazzled me in a remote way. When I asked about Susan, he plainly stated he had every faith he and Susan would eventually be reunited. To challenge this irksome confidence, I chatted promotingly about Juan, deleting my own new doubts about Juan's holiness.

I tried to discuss with Bill the significance of paying women to name-call him. Certainly he did not wish to examine the ramifications of these cheap tableaux vivants.

To give himself some more leverage in indulging perversity, Bill tried to convince me to have a hustler up to the apartment.

"Absolutely not," I said. "The idea doesn't interest me at all. I have no libido, and ultimately the poor fellow, I'm sure, would leave me with a very desolate feeling."

"Why? You could fantasize about him, pretend he's someone else. Hector, you wouldn't need to think about any discouraging aspects of it. I'd be paying. No money would pass your hands. We could even decide in advance who or what he's supposed to be before he walks in. Could even request a type similar to that Drake fellow you took a brief liking to."

"He's supposedly dead."

"But alive in a hustler double."

"What you're describing, Bill, is a pity fuck. A *double* pity fuck, since you'd be paying. Isn't it obvious I'm completely ill-equipped to accept any pity? An incorrect dose of pity would kill me on the spot."

"Silly, don't think of it in those dreary terms. Do you think I meditate on the lives of the women who kick me? No. When I go to a restaurant, do you think I'm thinking of the murder of the cow or the lamb or the cod? I'd only be able to order Jell-O then."

"Jell-O is made with an animal extract for the gelatin."

"Oh, shut up."

Bill went right ahead and hired the male prostitute. He lied to me that I had to be home for a special delivery he wouldn't be able to be present for—a "package," he said.

I suppose the Doorman was instructed to send him right up. He wasn't totally unpresentable. He wore one of those college-style overcoats with toggle buttons. Coat off, he was overwhelming, a lot of a good thing.

I was wearing a large, broadly knit cardigan sweater, and I gripped it closed like I was trapped in a snowstorm. He casually removed his upper garments, making some casual remark like "That's much better."

He didn't mind my nervous chatter and was surprisingly candid. He lived with his parents in Queens. They believed he was bartending at a fancy restaurant with no name. He had a young son who lived with his mother. He was making money to save up for his boy. Save up for what? I wondered.

He pressured me into nothing. He turned on the radio, searching briefly for a smooth jazz fusion thing, and then, unludicrously, began dancing around the room, smiling amiably, occasionally and very casually stroking his chest. He laughed a little bit, I guess to show he could see the humor in the situation.

He picked me up by the hand, hardly making much of a gesture, it was so smooth and easy. We danced slowly around the imposing end tables, sculptures, and uncomfortable chairs.

I started to weep a little; I couldn't help it. He petted my hair.

My mind raced ahead of me; I wanted to ruin it by spouting my detachment routine.

When the music changed we broke apart. He removed the rest of his garments. He'd shaved his body, and the smooth contours caught some afternoon light. I recoiled, knocking over one of the crazy gifts Susan's or Bill's parents had given them as a wedding present. It was an embroidery, framed on a standing easel. It had the short poem "Marriage" by Philip Larkin sewn into it. The poem went like this:

"My wife and I—we're *pals*. Marriage is *fun!*"
Yes: two can live as stupidly as one.

It's no wonder with wedding gifts like this that this home was packed with matrimonial disharmony—I mean adultery, prostitution, and perverse interactions with strangers. Oh, I'd chosen wisely when I got hooked up with the Deds! Anything wrong with me now was a spring day in the park by comparison.

"My name is Horatio," he said suddenly.

My name is Hamlet but my friends call me Ophelia, I thought to say. Names and more names. They're all just made up anyway. So idiotic.

Oh, can't he see that no kindness can help me now? No. Perhaps one mad florist could who would fill the room to capacity with purple hyacinths, white narcissi, red tulips, pink roses, yellow forsythia, pink quince, purple lilac, orange day lilies, yellow daffodils, red roses, wild daisies. . . .

(Get ahold of yourself!)

He has the finesse to orchestrate his ejaculation so its issue is caught in the palm of his hand.

I offer him the bathroom if he'd like to take a bath, but he said a friend who had just returned from Greece gave him a big sponge he's eager to use. I talked for a moment about my love of baths, joke that we have something in common, and then he is gone, Horatio.

At dinner at a nearby restaurant, Bill is very curious about it all. I suppose he needs his money's worth and, although I hate to lie for any reason, I expand the scenario to include more, let us say, physicality. Bill, devouring his mixed grill, is satisfied and begins bad-mouthing Kim's cooking and how he doesn't miss it.

"But I'll be having it again, I'm sure," he boasts.

"Why do you say that?"

"Because I have every faith Susan and I will be reunited."

Every faith.

"Matter of time," he adds.

Once again I can't identify what I've ordered. I don't even know which utensil it requires. It doesn't matter, since everything I eat burns in my stomach like a sour pickle. My theory is it's the medications burning through the walls of my stomach. I enjoy some strawberry ice cream. It's raining outside. I've tuned Bill out, his chatting on about his racquetball game, the racket that must be his job, the racket of whores and how he must "taper off" and promising he will.

What interests people? What career is so thrilling? If I were well, I would adopt a little disadvantaged baby and give it love. But it's so crazily difficult to adopt in this country I'd have to go to Mexico. Or else a little AIDS baby with a limited warranty, make its succeeding months less a hell. Yes, giving some amount of joy while here on earth must be our task. The spiritual uplifters all advocated *service*, but I'm too weak and tired to do service. And I feel guilty spending so much time prone on the bed. The quality of the sheets and the mattress have become an unnatural focus.

Maybe I should have chosen more wisely when I chose Susan and Bill to focus on away from my own blurry decay. When I imagine their faces in front of me, they're just projections of myself, I see that now. It probably isn't just the Deds but all the living who are merely mirrors of ourselves. I try to explain a few of these feelings to Bill and he listens thoughtfully, nodding his head and saying he admires the way I think.

I think it's hopeless. But I mustn't say so. I must play along. Detachment will come, it has to; it's just a race with the morphine drip to the finish.

This last week has gotten so much colder.

It turns out Juan is Puerto Rican and he has flown to old San Juan with Susan, so Bill and I visit the country house.

It is too much for my poor vision. I don't want to identify with things dropping dead around me even if they are gorgeous.

The scent of leaves burning sends me to the window. Bill's handsome face is ignited with a flicker as he circles the fiery heap, prodding it with a long stick.

The flames bring out his despair and drive. He has been rigorous in resurrecting the renovation of the house. A stone wall is being restored. Logs in the fireplaces. Moth-eaten but dry-cleaned blankets to throw over your legs. Susan's empty glasses are around the house, some with a drop of yet-to-be-evaporated water from the gone ice cube. Bill commands Kim to remove them. By the fire at night, Bill with his glass of Scotch and Kim in the kitchen making gingerbread men for tomorrow, I listen to Bill make some sentimental recollections which "humanize" him a bit. His sexual history postdating the gang rape of the professor's wife, innocent little stories of delayed satisfactions. He talks about discovering the full range of sensation in his penis, the variety of it. He is extremely explicit about sex with Susan; he gives her a lot of credit. He's nostalgic for his missing ball.

I cannot be enticed into sharing flashbacks—quite simply, I don't feel like remembering. I remember too much. Stories must have beginnings and endings. The beginning of this and the end of that. Fucking the Man with the Silver Attaché Case, cash steaming, filthy ass. Begin this. End that. Names and places. Beach house. Someone's rental, a share, alcoholic ex-model up at 8:00 a.m. to mix Campbell's beef bouillon into her vodka, "for my throat."

Something pretty to tell.

Little delicate Kim has found a fellow androgyne and they are in love. An eighteenth-century plate I'd admired once in a museum depicted a damsel and a wastrel, hand in hand, walking among the blooming apple trees. Kim and John were very much like this walking, also hand in hand, among the crazed leaves jumping to earth. I saw them kiss tenderly in the pantry. When I expressed approval and admiration for their fond love, they informed me very solemnly they would be getting married before long.

John wasn't always there. He patrolled a little squadron of much rougher-looking boys and they would all do assorted lawn work. The rough boys didn't like to work, and many wouldn't show up as scheduled, making John look bad. Although I knew nothing about this and believed flowering plants just sprouted up of their own accord, it was bulb-planting season, and John and the boys spent many hours burying the onionlike balls in the earth to provide for their spring appearance. There were one thousand of them.

One small near-catastrophe involved a huge, healthy pot plant Bill was growing on the property. Ever since the house had been purchased Bill had been mothering the robust stalk, counting the months until he could harvest the beloved buds. Well, someone hacked it off at its base and stole it!

I have never seen Bill so upset (except about his ball), and he stormed right over to John and, without accusing him, demanded he retrieve the stolen marijuana plant from whichever sleazy hired hand had hacked it. "You will lose this account!" Bill said, and added more ominously, "And perhaps Kim too." Not five hours later the plant appeared, a little tired from the trip but still asking to be dried, rolled, and smoked. Bill was very satisfied with himself and reiterated to John that though he trusted *him,* he would have to hold him wholly responsible for whomever he brought onto the property. The only truly unpleasant moment was when Kim innocently asked if they should call the police to trace down the theft and Bill shouted, "No, you *fool!*"

The windows are no longer secure in their casements, and at night they rattle spookily, as if the house were calling back its previous tenants. I pile blankets on myself and can see the moon from where I'm lying. It's cantaloupe-colored and egalitarian as it lights Kim and John scrunching through a midnight walk.

Shush reappeared. Bill summoned her to lick his wounds. (The cupidity in the pantry ultimately depressed him.)

Shush said she was very changed now, pursuing a second college education. Like Bill, she had been thrown out and dropped out of various institutions, enthusiastic about sports, the opposite sex, and beach events. To build credence or look like Judy Holliday, she now donned thick black-framed glasses. I think I was supposed to have complete

amnesia of the old Shush and discuss serious subjects with the new one. Most serious subjects were
pre-empted by her campaign to win my vote advo-
cating the union of her and Bill. She didn't know
why Bill was so vague about the divorce proceed-
ings, but assured me repeatedly she could be a
"healing force" in Bill's chaotic "marital war."

"Did you ever feel you would die young?" she
asked.

"Well, I'm not dead yet, and I'm not so young."

"Yeah, but life must really feel finished for you
with all remaining emphasis on feeble medical
treatments." Her philosophical tone was intolerable
and comical, but she wasn't so far from the truth.
Hearing her review my state aloud, I had to admit
it was realistic. What really was left? Unless some
miracle cure or booster arrived, I couldn't expect
much. She reminded me how obvious my bad situation was, and her simplicity made the obviousness
of it embarrassing. It was embarrassing to be sick,
embarrassing to die.

I took comfort in that she was something of a
bigot, criticizing Kim and John. She nagged Bill
about it, how "unnatural" it was, an "unsavory"
presence. He shut her up by simply shouting,
"Leave go of it already, I say!"

To make herself seem domestic, she invaded the
kitchen with her grandmother's recipe for "Bruns-
wick Stew," a mucky trough of unidentifiable meats
and vegetables. I criticized the big raw potatoes in
it and she blew up. What right had I to criticize? she
said pointedly. None, I admitted.

But I preferred the little bits of drama to total stasis in my room. I'd become a melodrama junkie, moving around a limited number of characters, switching often: today Susan, tomorrow Bill; Juans and Shushes, good-hearted prostitutes, Susan and Bill's heterosexual friends—all satirical, edgy—and then the backdrop of people dropping dead, bodies thumping to the floor; I grew to need war reports as well as frivolous nonsense. One of Noh's closest friends, an actress in some deliberately ridiculous theater company, died yesterday, covered in purple spots and withered hideously. "I'm glad," I said defensively. "I'm glad her suffering's over. Horrifying but relatively fast."

If Shush wanted to give her *Mad* magazine versions of Immanuel Kant and Simone Weil over foul dinner, fine, *great.* If Bill refused to sleep with her and you could hear her halfway into the night whining to be let into his bedroom and let her *try*— fine, *great.* If Susan's sentimental life had been exchanged for the most ready form of sensuality— hurray! I just hope I have never been too obstructive to anyone's wheel of distractions. We'll even buy your ticket, but do observe the rules. Bright smiles and all that.

My sleeping pill isn't working. My bad eye seems more bad tonight.

Even tonight there is too much darkness. Clouds or fog have wiped out the stars, and that harvest moon I'd admired has become a veil dancer, critical and fleeting.

Is it Kim and John I hear laughing downstairs?

They sound like Flora and Miles in *The Turn of the Screw*. Eerie joy. They don't trust me very much. I must represent some old order. But what order is that?

My religious reading kept me returning to the principle of absolute zero; but could this world ever properly present *absolute zero*? It could provide Dachau, lilies of the valley, shortbread, bad food, fur coats, first love, lakes at sunset, pearls, lynchings, comets; but could it ever present the absolute zero? Perhaps the atomic bomb was the closest thing— God's personality full-blown. The geometry of suffering is like some awful advanced math problem you couldn't figure out on your final exam. The proctor is very passive about it; he says, "Don't worry—everyone fails."

The sun is coming up—that was fast! I hear Bill shout from his bedroom, an ecstatic shout. He has had his first "normal" orgasm since his operation. Shush has somehow managed to worm her way into his nest of shame and freed him of his final inhibition, to be seen with one ball—a modern Adam, no longer a threat to his gender, a red rooster croaking at the rise of the sun. Shush, after all her cooing, has fallen silent, exhausted, triumphant, sleepy.

Pabst said, "Luuissssse, after lunch you must cry." I said, "Okay, after lunch I will cry." So then we went back on the set and I cried. It was never any problem.

LOUISE BROOKS

—

Youthtrap Monkey/
Bain-Marie

Let's all laugh.

Sincerely.

I'd promised you I would never send you back to the hospital. It isn't as if we lied to you; they just came to take you away.

It's funny, though, your longing for detachment now that you've attained pure detachment. Detachment of the eye. Retinal detachment. We couldn't have planned it better if we'd placed an ad in the papers: "Detachment freaks seek operations in which detachable body parts of a preferably tender nature are cut and sewn."

Why "we"?

Schizophrenics and prostitutes often refer to themselves in the third person: "She feels real tonight." I use the word "we" here to suggest the plurality of madness. The clutter of voices sitting at the edge of my bed has made us quite cuckoo. I will return to "I" when eye can see again. Currently we are in bandages and there is only blackness and unidentifiable voices.

The operation itself went very smoothly. A competent doctor cut into the eye and inserted the same kind of silicone disc used for breast implants, only much smaller. There are tiny Frankensteinian stitches across the upper corner of the left eye. Both eyes, however, are covered. The stitches will dissolve, they say, in a month.

"Hector, it's me, Aunt Mica. Do you remember me?"

We don't know an Aunt Mica. Go away.

She is at the bottom edge of the bed touching our feet.

Someone has joined her or else there's a second bed in the room with its own visitors.

"Charles, I'm not going to let you blame your whole life on me. It isn't fair."

Is the TV on?

"Who out there knows what a bain-marie is?"

"Isn't it the water Marie leaves in the tub after a bath?"

"No."

"It's similar to a court-bouillon, only the bouquet garni is replaced with a secret ingredient from any young girl named Marie."

"No. Haven't we heard enough nonsense? Any cook knows a bain-marie is simply a pan or pot of water in which a second pan containing food is semi-submerged to slow down the cooking process or to keep the already prepared food warm."

"When your mother finally told us you had AIDS, we wanted to rush right over, but we didn't want to make you self-conscious. Then when we heard you were at this hospital ten feet from our building, how could we not stop in and say hello?"

"If out of poor judgment or reckless cooking, your bain-marie is deeper than it ought to be, then water will flood over your mashed potatoes or custard and ruin it. Food is a substance that can be ruined, sooner than reputations, sooner than the face. The journeyman who thinks he can cook without regard to technique is embarking on a race down a dark tunnel of mishaps."

We had the doctor, nurse, and interns play an ashram cassette during the operation. This was against their better judgment, as they preferred Michael Jackson. The pleasant chanting, we believe, lent some serenity during the splicing.

It was afterward, in the room (a room without a toilet costing in excess of one thousand dollars a night) that our skull began its multipurpose cracking. Behind our eyes a coup was going on, and

megaphones abreast of the casualties kept repeating, "We are all going down."

"Phyllis, three of my best friends' husbands have
left them for younger women—not simultaneously
but consecutively. Are we only our looks, Phyllis?
Are we only our bodies? I'm an educated person,
like you, and I have years of opinions to give. But
now I'm supposed to readjust my whole position in
society as something discarded?"

"Is Peter leaving you?"

"Did I say that? My subconscious said it. It
knows more than I do and is preparing me for the
big abandonment."

"Ali MacGraw has this cable program with some
other women about makeup. Of course they're trying to sell their makeup, but they also tell life stories
that support the need for better, longer-lasting
makeup. Ali MacGraw said that she had no self-
esteem while married to Steve McQueen. And it was
even worse when she was with the head of Para-
mount. Makeup, in a way, saved her, gave her back
her face."

"During one of my lucid evenings I explained to
Cosmos the concept of the youthtrap monkey.
'What's that?' he says. 'It goes something like this.
You, Cosmos, have a new and younger girlfriend
every six months. How an old bag like you gets
them is another story I don't know, but it's an addiction, Cosmos, that's clear. You know how they describe the addict as having a monkey on his back?
Well, that's your monkey, Cosmos. You wait and see

how the youthtrap closes in on you. See, I've given up on all that—sure, I look like hell, but I'm not waiting to have the last laugh, because I'm laughing now.'"

"Hector, are you in much pain? Do your eyes burn?"

"Noh? Noh, is that you?"

"It's your friend Drake. Maxwell. Remember me?"

"Aren't you dead?"

"Yes, but that's okay. I wanted to say hello. Everything is really *okay*. It's so freeing, Hector, to have no desires left! You have no idea how free! I can't wait until you join us. It'll be the most pleasant surprise you've ever had. Big kiss."

A ducklike voice says, "I do my own bain-marie, but I do it in the bathroom. I run a warm tub and place a smaller tub within the larger tub. Then I squeeze my bottom into the smaller one and fart as many times as I can. I may even release a bit of shit. It's my own version of the court-bouillon. I completely eliminate the need for a bouquet garni."

"Hector, it's Uncle Donovan. Do you remember me? I always knew you were queer, but I was too timid to tell you I was too! That was so selfish of me! I could have made you feel less alone. Forgive me please."

The decorator of infinite elegance says elimination elimination elimination. We must silence the voices that congest the perfect decor of solitude.

"Who do you identify with more, Veronika Voss or Petra von Kant?"

"What? Who are they?"

"Fassbinder heroines, you dodo."

"Fassbinder?"

"German film director, baby. Died at thirty-six, just like Marilyn. See, you've already outlived them."

I felt a lump of wool thrown across my legs.

"Hector, here's the Missoni sweater I borrowed six years ago and never returned. I didn't want you to die with me owing you anything. The purple sweater."

An old witch once told me that by repeating a phrase or expression over and over you could turn it into a curse or a magic spell. You could use it to travel very far in your mind. Just repeat.

Bain-marie, bain-marie, bain-marie . . .

You are in a beautiful beach hotel. A private house turned hotel. French doors open out onto a slate deck. Steps down to the sea. Opalescent and warm to the touch. You make love—hungry, clean love. The sun is pink. The sand is wheat. Dinner is champagne. Words are hardly exchanged, longings extinguished like candles.

Bain-marie, bain-marie, bain-marie . . .

Towers of snow, violet colored, five o'clock, red lips, bells, destinations . . .

The curse can work both ways, though. It can turn on you and ugly Mrs. Terrorist, the fourth-grade teacher, is isolating each of the students she can not tolerate. Pacheco, the one dark-skinned student in the class, she separates his desk so he is in an aisle by himself. Vale she sends out on a ruse and tells the rest of the class to avoid him and by all means never befriend him, for he will grow up to be a criminal. Open School Week she tells my mother I'm worthless at punchball in the pebbles during lunch hour when she watches from her high window and makes blackboard notes of who is naughty and who is not nice. . . .

"You don't know who Petra von Kant is, my dear? Why, she is every homosexual rolled into one. *The Bitter Tears of*—"

"I don't think so."

"You don't think so? You merely need look in a mirror."

Outside it must be raining again. It's going to be a rainy Halloween. Our pillow is wet with sweat. Something furry has jumped on our pillow and crawled up near our ear.

"Hello."

"Who are you?"

"Monkey."

"That's your name?"

"Part of it."

"You've come to give some kind of warning?"

"Maybe."

The creature sticks its tongue deep down into our mouths. We're gagging on this blind French kiss. The monkey hair tickles and nauseates us.

It backs off and speaks.

"Where are your dreams now, sweetie? Could they be here, or here, or perhaps in a vial in the laboratory? Let's hold the glass slide smeared with your dreams up to the light. Goodness! It's an invasion of nasty things—ambitions, ideals, presumptions. . . . Do the monkey. Come on, do the monkey!"

"In *The Bitter Tears of Petra von Kant* a lesbian fashion designer falls very heavily for a female model who is basically heterosexual. The devotion is deeply masochistic. Spurned by the callous model, Petra spits on the compassion offered by her mother, daughter, friend, and secretary. After Petra stomps on a tea set with her silver platform shoes, the model shows up in a conciliatory mood, but Petra simply says, 'It's too late.'

"In *Veronika Voss* a retired, drug-addicted ex-actress from the Nazi-controlled German film industry gains the curious attentions of a sportswriter. He learns Veronika is under the control of the iron-fisted directress of a very private sanatorium where patients of a certain ilk report for their illegal fixes. The directress, a lesbian, in the end locks Veronika in a small hospitallike room in the sanatorium and then leaves, presumably on vacation with her all-girl staff. Veronika is left to die an agonized cold-turkey death. At some point she muses how strange death must be, but then she catches herself and says contemptuously, 'Ah, life is strange too!'

"Aside from their extreme bleakness both films are riddled with lesbian stereotypes. Must homosexuals forever be depicted as some evil lice? Must we perpetuate misery—myths that service the many who practice hate against homosexuals? Or could these be exemplary tales to mock the farfetched and demented notion that homosexuality is a 'lifestyle'?

Who but a mad person would pick such a punishing 'style'? And are all things the majority finds distasteful merely 'styles': serial murders, spouse battering, corruptions in the judicial system? Could the world be *that* stylish?"

"Noh, is that you? Tell me. I can't see you."

"Fassbinder doesn't stop there. He casts himself in the lead of his film *Fox and His Friends*, in which, as yet another jilted gay person, he is thoroughly beaten up in a subway station. I'd rest my case, but it's just an old Kelly bag."

"Hector, it's Aileen, Aileen and Bob. Are you in horrible pain?"

"Where's Susan? Is Susan here?"

"No, Susan isn't here. You haven't heard? She's been abducted."

"Abducted? By whom?"

"The Monkey!"

"What monkey? Juan?"

"No. The *Monkey*. I thought you would have at least heard about it on the news. It's the youthtrap you keep hearing about closing in on a whole new generation."

"You mean dying young?"

"Well, not necessarily to be put in a casket. The death can be quite lingering. It wouldn't be much of a trap if it didn't permit you to twist around for a while within its grip."

"It's just an idea, it's not real! Bob, tell him."

"Bill wanted to be here, but he got a promotion, so he had to make a good show at the office."

"A promotion? What does he do?"

"Oh, look—someone's throwing up on this cooking show! Sometimes I just love disgusting things, because they have the weird ability to get your mind off your troubles. Should I tell the most disgusting thing I can think of? Bob's date, before we were married, with an heiress? Ooh, I won't say her name. Bob, you tell it."

"You tell it, Aileen—you tell it so well."

"Well, it's very short. First she stole Bob's car. Then she got Bob horribly drunk—I think he might have thrown up on her, and to get revenge, after Bob passed out, she left a big steaming turd on his chest! Isn't that disgusting?!"

"We're talking through masks, Hector, because of the TB epidemic. Be careful, Hector—don't French-kiss anyone while you're here!"

There's a shift from the bed to a stretcher on wheels. We're wheeling down the corridors.

"I'm sorry, Mr. Diaz, we're moving you to the Dead Ward."

"What? I'm not dead yet!"

"No, but the Hopeless Ward has gotten far too crowded this evening. It might be only temporary. Don't worry, there'll be a lot of other Spanish-speaking people in there with you."

"I'm not Spanish."

"Well, whatever."

Monkey whips its tail across my face and says, "Told you so—told you so."

Prayer must never be answered: if it is, it ceases
to be prayer and becomes correspondence.

OSCAR WILDE

———

Kim's Wedding

Kim's wedding, I swear to you, was no hallucination. Its reality was preceded by such elaborate
preparation as to challenge creation itself in fecund
invention. You may guess mass boredom brews a
mad surge of alternative energy. You may point to
Petronius's *Satyricon* to understand an earlier wedding of two young boys. Since the guest list was
eclectic to an extreme, perhaps it could be surmised
this was a strong cross-section of disenchanted
Americans. Although the government had tried and
failed to jolt the citizens into shame and conformity,
families continued to dissolve like sugar in water,

couples as quickly. Television, I was told, had become more repressive. Smart, alert children were the new gods, and their products the only thing hoisting up the flaccid economy.

I was in the hospital much longer than you realize. That stupid DDI I was taking damaged my pancreas, so that these knifelike pains I'd complained about earlier were not from eating seasoned food but pancreatitis. My own doctor had persisted in suggesting antacids for the pain (at one hundred dollars a visit); but in the hospital, eyes wrapped blind, I moaned about my stomach, they felt around and took a blood test to rate my amylase count, and declared my latest ailment. The addictive painkiller Percocet offered no particular high.

I was on that ugly bridge where you've walked too far and the bridge is warped, soggy, just little strips of bamboo, and the whole thing shakes and swings a little when you breathe too close to it.

I've arranged with the psychiatrist the pills and the suppositories. I only need to secure the plastic-bag tier. He's suddenly very afraid he may be incriminated in connection with my using the lethal painkillers. Everyone knows what the drug is used for, but pharmacists are not reluctant to fill the prescription for AIDS patients. After all, they must think, what damn difference should it make now? I've hidden the lethal drugs.

I spent a great deal of energy and time combing the country house for a place where workmen would not interfere. It was nice, rediscovering this haunted house in the process of being haunted by—what?—the new? I was too lethally sophisticated myself to believe that God would permit anything new on the Green Planet. He'd done so much, and so much that replenished itself so unbegrudgingly, he'd certainly not bother now with revision. Human beings were reflections of himself, and he had his own astonishing vanities. One need only observe the developments in physics to see the infinite indifference of fortune. Solar systems are explored and the astronaut curtly informed he could never be welcome at that party—"frozen out," I think the expression goes. A little girl named Annabelle told me at the party that everything that doesn't feed the mind eats the mind. And Annabelle is only seven, with little anachronistic ribbons in her hair.

I am impressed with the large number of so-called ordinary people who have shown up to create this highly ornamental celebration. That people who give up their Saturday to drive to this house are willing to twirl bits of paper or stuff little canape shells, and not complain or get bored, is a miracle. In fact, the house, after hours of decoration, looked very much like the site of a miracle, with garlands of both natural and handmade flowers draped in every main-floor room from corner to corner. The sheer quantity of all these flowers, real and artificial, joined by tinted-foil cutouts from a holiday stencil book, put the party out of time and season.

Mag was able to induce her entire staff to appear with their children, spouses, former spouses, and just friends. Some very dynamic couple who run a catering company went to work amassing huge piles of chicken salad. They were amicably bossy and got a dozen people to chop, peel, and toss. Restaurant-quality machinery stood proudly over carrot salad and celery-apple-nut salad; the potato salad was an herb picker's delight.

The house must have entertained frequently in its past; pitchers of every shape, size, color, and humor were ready for fruity punches. Everything fit in the restaurant-style refrigerators that had been ordered and installed some few weeks ago, ample waiting ground for their impending relief effort.

Although everyone was racing around in jovial industry (with the exception of the very young children, who contributed by twirling, clapping, and giggling deliciously), I sat in an overstuffed chair covered in an array of ancient (but clean) cotton blankets.

I wasn't "helping," but I was somehow made to feel very much a part of the wedding preparations. No one asked me how-was-I-feeling-type questions, so I was kindly spared my obvious invalid status. Instead I was urged to eat little tidbits, ostensibly to give an opinion on their flavor. Similarly, I was shown decorations and paper lanterns for approval.

I couldn't for a moment that afternoon think about death. Life had reached a fairy-tale status in this house on this day, and I simply could not believe the enthusiasm of this wide variety of people who ordinarily would not comprehend, condone, or conspire toward an extravagant marriage of two boys—or a modest one, either. Was everyone fully cognizant of this union?

Kim and John were intentionally absent the whole day, not that the celebration should be a surprise but so that they not be in the way of what one worker described as "the evening explosion of joy." They were off taking in a bunch of movies at the mall.

Susan rented matching sky-blue tuxedos for them. Yes, a pink carnation in either lapel.

Juan was there with a pack of friends he'd never mentioned. The energy between Susan and Juan had dissipated, but neither were there any unfriendly feelings to detect.

Shush spotted Juan and, ignited by his virile good looks, ran to his side to discuss the fruit salad she'd been put in charge of. He showed so little interest in her lichees and winter melons that she, discouraged, moseyed over to my encampment, pulled up a chair, and made small talk surprisingly free of ad hoc medical advice.

You understand I'd grown so tired of explaining all the therapies—the "successful" ones and the flops. People were suddenly respecting the plain ole deathliness of the situation.

The only person who said something nutty was the priest who was to perform the nuptials. "Praying for you to pull through!" he said. Pull through what? Come on, as of this cold December, *there is no cure*. But the badly inebriated guy had to be forgiven; he'd agreed to perform this unorthodox service and hardly raised a drunken eyebrow in protest. "Bless you all," he said, to his credit.

Shush, gabbing next to me as she skinned the hairy lichees, still maintained some delusion about her relationship with Bill. She assured me she'd saved him from the deepest mire of promiscuity. But she'd turned wise to the fact she'd better not go on any anti-Susan tract, that it would get her nowhere.

Before exiting to the kitchen, Shush sang this piece of advice to me, probably lifted from some movie: "Boys who come to tea can't expect to stay for dinner."

I didn't care so much. I wasn't really reconciled with either Susan or Bill. I had a strong sense they'd abandoned me. My hopeless state mirrored too much their own. They were a funny contrast today of their usual selves. Susan had a big Auntie Em apron on and was running around as if she were the head of a vital relief effort. Bill behaved as if his only son were getting married and the event marked a personal success in his own development.

They seemed like just anyone else in the room. I couldn't even detect any marks of hostility. Maybe they'd forgotten everything or forgiven or were just delirious with Kim's wedding. Even Bill's Bad Boy Club members were there, drinking Scotch and sodas, I might emphasize, but also hanging Christmas lights outside and inside the house. I'd had someone put up a sign at the Let's-Do-Nothing Club, something like: GLORIOUS LIFE-AFFIRMING UNMIXED MARRIAGE—BRING DECORATIONS! There were directions what train to take and all that. A group showed up together, but I didn't know a one of them. The ones I half-knew I half-knew were dead.

This is something I hadn't anticipated as I approached the end: how depressing it would be.

Oh, I could joke about this or that and find people earnestly flailing at their work a big burlesque. I could even laugh at myself (easy!).

But now . . .

I would be joining the haunted dining room where you are recollected as someone's brief love, as someone's spoiled child, as someone so critical his comeuppance is to be a ghost no more or less refined than any other phantom.

If Susan and Bill should ever have a child (at present not likely, unless they use a ten-foot pole), I can imagine the angelic child one rainy afternoon going through a rarely touched drawer and finding some photographs and examining them. Pictures of me. Pictures of me with Susan. Pictures of me with Bill.

"Mother," the child asks, "who is this? Is this Uncle Hector?"

"This is just an old friend of Mommy's and Daddy's. Someone who vanished."

"Vanished? People are still looking for him?"

"No."

"He's dead."

"That's the word people use, but really everyone is just hiding, and in the end we're all going to pop out and scream 'Surprise!'"

Around this time the front door flew open and

there stood two sky-blue grooms. They were surrounded by their ushers, the ruffians who were expressly forbidden to attend but, look at them, they'd really made an attempt at playing their parts. They'd unearthed their fathers' (or grandfathers') wedding costumes and stood pridefully erect in twisted cummerbunds, elephant bell-bottoms, and pleated shirts in apricot, lime, banana, and, of course, shocking pink.

The room fell utterly silent for longer than a moment, and then someone shouted either "Hurray!" or "Hurry!," I don't know which.

And then a big boom of music began. It took some time to adjust the volume, but in the interim the jolly drunken priest danced down an aisle he created himself by making high kicks, clicking his heels in the air, and swinging his arms above his red head.

Now I knew why everyone was so cooperative working all day in this house. They would be given the honor of dancing in a madhouse. It was worth the longish drive, the cutting-up of little things with scissors you were instructed to carry from home, the skinning of grapefruit sections, the hooking-up of light and sound systems, the endless destemming of the tarragon leaves for the minced chicken salad.

When the party seemed the least "real," a woman who'd hired a van to fill with out-of-season flowers at 8:30 a.m. in the Manhattan flower district and now stood with her residue—violets, tea roses, lilies of the valley laced around her like a perfumer's web—shouted, "THIS IS REAL!"

I could not challenge her. I was seeing no less than my own dream come true. A thing unblemished by even a passing glance from the flesh markets. A backdrop conceived and executed by Blake, Disney, and Cocteau, all drunk on the same fruit punch.

Sure, it's exhilarating to see your own wishes materialized, if not for you at least for someone else (Kim? John!), but it's also frightening and lonely. I know it's disgusting to feel pity for yourself, so I tried to change my mood by picturing the whole wedding party as skeletons with lipstick and purple sausages. That worked only for a few seconds.

I guess, somehow, while I was sleigh-riding around in my head, the boys were married, food was passed around, games played, dancing, cake cutting.

I couldn't shake my fog. Children circled me. I made some clown faces and was funny and they all became my friends immediately. (What a contrast from my own childhood.)

Some of the children interviewed me.

A little person named Charles stepped forward. "Do you think the two boys who got married were really boys, or was one a girl?"

"Well," I said thoughtfully, "unless we see their peepees I guess we'll never know!" This was a hit in terms of baby talk and logic.

"My mother says you're going to die but that I can give you a kiss and I won't catch anything."

"A kiss!" I said, mock-scandalized. "Why, we only

just met! We'd have to go on a few dates first, but since your mother knows I'm going to die, I guess we won't have time to really get to know one another. It's a pity. But maybe you'll remember me."

You think that the dead don't smell nice. I know. When the cider's boiling, it smells like a wet cow-stall. Death's like cider—it's got to throw off its scum!

———

Sunyata

"Sunyata" means Nothingness. It said so in a chain letter that came today.

They had a colorized version of *A Christmas Carol* on last night, but I would mute the sections I didn't care for with the remote control. I don't like when they show him making all the wrong choices in life and turning into a lonely coot. I don't so much mind the beginning, when he's uniformly mean to everyone, but that's because I love the end, when he becomes overjoyed with transformational love. Then I turn the sound up and cry.

There's no sense crying now, right? So late in the day.

I didn't mention you, did I? I'm sorry. I meant to, in a way. You helped me, but I hated needing help. And then I got very involved thinking about S. and B.'s marriage.

Who should I have loved? You? Or you? I would have had to let you look at me. Like this. You don't know what I look like now. A branch from a burnt tree.

What did you expect of me? What?—gratitude? I just wanted to *forget* . . . like everyone else. Forget for a little while and have a laugh! Then, as you know, it became impossible. It all wasn't much fun then. Not for me and not for you.

You. You. You. You're all mad at me now. I didn't describe the day I craved black cherries and you got them. And massaged my feet.

Or you who told me not to burn this pile of notes. I'd called Noh about the notes I'd been keeping and he screamed, "Burn them! Burn everything!" He'd just been to another memorial service and was singing, ". . . Nine urns of ashes, eight creaking caskets, seven pals a-perishing, six cronies croaking . . ." etc.

I remembered Noh's name! I hadn't been able to remember my own name. Someone called who needed "the names of the residents of this residency." I said, "Gee, I dunno," and hung up.

Two little birds were singing on the window sill and I called to them, "Hi, little birds!" and they flew away.

Is it a sin to forget everybody? To void so many people who went to the trouble of being themselves? But they'll die too. And it won't so much be that we'll all be together as that it won't matter.

No mirrors in my room. I had them removed. Vampire.

Santa wrote me a special letter this year.

Dear Hector:

    I've had a long talk (actually not so long) with God and we've decided not to give you any presents this Christmas. This decision is based on many years of observing your cool ingratitude for countless inventive toys from Toyland and beautiful sweaters from Heaven. So, Mr. Picky, you won't have to worry about unwrapping a lot of stuff to be critical of this or any other forthcoming year! And to answer any zany questions you might have asked had you taken the trouble to correspond with us—if God should decide to continue the sporadic practice of reincarnation, you should most certainly return as a gecko in an unbearable climate. This brief note terminates this and all further communication with Santa and Santa Industries—not to be confused in your sick mind with Satan who I'm sure you'd like to blame for all your ungodly twists in the road of Life. God bless those who still get presents!

    Decidedly,
    Santa Claus

I decided not to let this letter bother me. Besides, I heard Meister Eckhart in the hall, his little wood-soled fourteenth-century slippers.

He offered me a lot of encouraging words and polite admonishments about not adhering to despair. He looked a lot like my grandfather in a three-piece gray suit and dark hat. It could have been my grandfather beckoning me to the other side (for all my bags were packed), but the funny shoes gave him away as the Meister.

I prayed. *Bless me. Santa and his devils cannot lead me to the red chamber of Doubt. I have come so far, God, you cannot dump me now.*

The snow falling outside seemed not to observe the walls, and it snowed, room temperature, around my dizzy head.

The bare trees, needless to say, are a comfort. Everything I observe is invested with holiness, I need only suck the fear out of it. The bureau, the nightstand, the little bookshelf of decaying books—I bless each one, and a kind of Hans Christian Andersen thing happens and they move and reassure me with love.

The more I can saturate the room with love, the more present God will become.

I can't swallow anymore, so I don't eat.

How pure!

They want to put me in the hospital to nourish and hydrate me, but I've refused. Susan and Bill (I think it was them) have stood behind me. No food, no shit.

My involuntary twitching is an impromptu homage to the approach of angels. Their own fluttering I see only as good news—literal, not symbolic, as real as oatmeal. Angels of every size and color, sympathetic, telepathic, exquisite.

I think I made you up inside my head.

SYLVIA PLATH

———

Leaving So Soon?

My face is down in the dirt. Outdoors. Just how I knew it would be, ha-ha. Having sworn off medical incarceration, I am at the January house, where new beginnings disembark.

I've yanked out my arm catheter and the vein drools blood. Should I not tell you that? Should I resurrect the supremacy of the hyacinth, entreat the purple lamb to purr? This is my last chance to be accurate; permit me a little blood.

My face has broken the surface of a thin sheet of ice over a little puddle. The spider-web flower the break makes is further proof beauty presides over this function. My good eye revolves around in its socket in search of the arrival of souls. The living and the dead. I'm not choosy. The hurricane of choices is over; all knots of icy wind are accepted as good weather.

I've accepted Susan and Bill. I saw them walk hand in hand near the house. I did!

Once I was in a garden.

Susan and I had both managed to get into a summer arts colony. The usual array of sad sacks and overnight sensations crowded the baronial dining hall. But beyond the dining and the bring-your-own-bottle imbibing there was a splendid rose garden. I mean famous; tourists were permitted to enter the private sanctioned garden during the warm months.

The quality of the intense velvety red—almost purple—roses was dazzling. At twilight the garden regained its privacy, and guests of the colony were, though permitted to stroll the lanes of highly pruned blooms, strictly forbidden to cut the enflamed roses. The scent and the soft petting of the petals was enough for us. To inhale intoxication more completely as the moon and the darkness ate up the rivalrous color, we lay down on the cool earth—she on her back, me on my stomach—and we honored the genus.

Another summer, not too long afterwards, the garden was a ruin of stubs with thorns. A frost had come that winter and destroyed the vital roses. It was a scene of devastation, and I fell to the ground, this time in fear and mourning. That afternoon I'd gotten a letter informing me Keith had died of that "new" disease. I rose and ran to the nearby lake, circled the lake as it began to rain, running, thinking of tying a rock to my leg and sinking in the green, sticky water. I knew then I was earmarked for a horrible frost. As the color flushed from my face, I believe, there I attained detachment. It was detachment or the bottom of the lake.

And here I'd been pursuing it like a bandit for his loot when in fact I was rich with it. Now, through reverse geography (running backwards), I've attained some level of atonement, enlightened if only to see nature's face more clearly, its sharp distaste for longevity but its furry admiration for endurance.

My face is down in the dirt, but make no mistake, it is a beautiful place. Even the little bowls of bread soaked in milk Kim has left near the oak tree for me only enhance the landscape which is God's presence. Even the dead flowers must be groomed and honored, and by leaving them we leave death, and those are the attachments of this world. Fear be gone! Please do not feel sorry for me—I go to some place thrilling!

> Listen then to this wonder! How wonderful it is to be both outside and inside, to seize and to be seized, to see and at the same time to be what is seen, to hold and to be held—*that* is the goal where the spirit remains at rest, united with our dear eternity.
>
> MEISTER ECKHART

A NOTE ON THE TYPE

This book was set in a digitized version of a type face called Baskerville. The face itself is a facsimile reproduction of types cast from molds made for John Baskerville (1706–1775) from his designs. Baskerville's original face was one of the forerunners of the type style known to printers as "modern face"—a "modern" of the period A.D. 1800.

Composed by Graphic Composition, Inc.,
Athens, Georgia

Printed and bound by Arcata / Fairfield,
Fairfield, Pennsylvania

Design by Dorothy Schmiderer Baker

JameS
1312 4388587